WE BOTH READ®

Thing and Stop-It
Parent's Introduction

Whether your child is a beginning reader, a reluctant reader, or an eager reader, this book offers a fun and easy way to encourage and help your child in reading.

Similar to most We Both Read books, this book is designed for a parent and child to take turns reading aloud. It features dialog between two characters. The cat's dialog is designed be read aloud by a parent (or a child who is a fluent reader), and the dialog for the puppy is designed to be read by a beginning reader.

Depending on your child's reading skills, you may want to read the entire book to your child before reading it together. As you read, try to make the story come alive by reading with expression. This will help to model good fluency and make the book more engaging.

Some words that might be challenging for your child to read are introduced in the cat's dialog, distinguished with **bold** lettering. Pointing out and discussing these words can help to build your child's reading vocabulary.

It may be very helpful to point at the word bubbles as each of you reads and even run a finger under the dialog as it is being read. When you point at the puppy's word bubbles, which have a light blue background and slightly larger text, your child will know it is his or her turn to read.

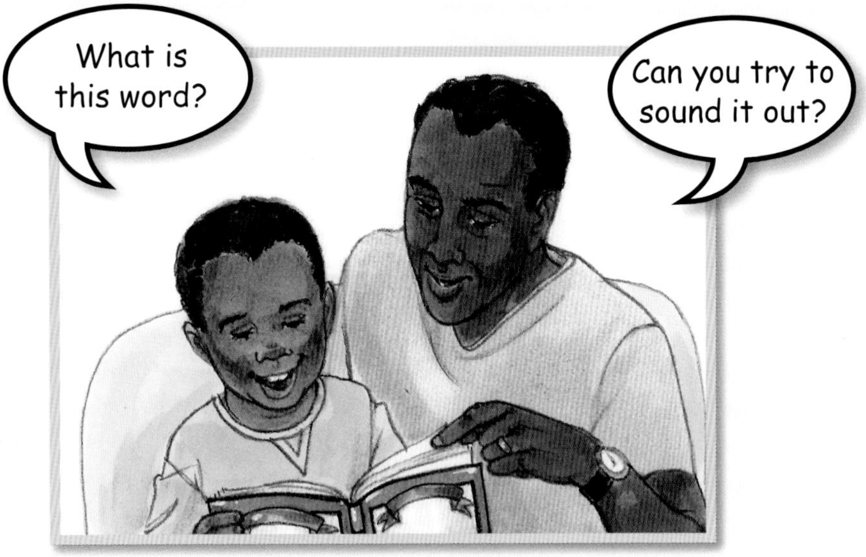
What is this word?
Can you try to sound it out?

If your child struggles with a word, you can encourage "sounding it out," but keep in mind that not all words can be sounded out. Your child might pick up clues about a word from the picture, other words in the sentence, or a word you just previewed in your reading. If your child struggles with a word for more than five seconds, it is usually best to simply say the word.

Most of all, remember to praise your child's efforts and keep the reading fun. Rereading this book multiple times may also be helpful for your child, and after several readings your child may want to read the entire book.

Try to keep the tips above in mind as you read together, but don't worry about doing everything right. Simply sharing the enjoyment of reading together will increase your child's reading skills and help start your child off on a lifetime of reading enjoyment!

Thing and Stop-It

A We Both Read Graphic Novel
Level 1
Puppy: Guided Reading Level E
Cat: Guided Reading Level L

Text Copyright © 2021 by Sindy Mckay
Illustrations Copyright © 2021 by Leo Trinidad
All rights reserved

We Both Read® is a registered trademark of Treasure Bay, Inc.

Published by
Treasure Bay, Inc.
P.O. Box 119
Novato, CA 94948 USA

Printed in Malaysia

Library of Congress Control Number: 2020941816

ISBN: 978-1-60115-366-1

Visit us online at:
WeBothRead.com

PR-11-20

Thing and Stop-It

By Sindy McKay

Family Engagement in Reading

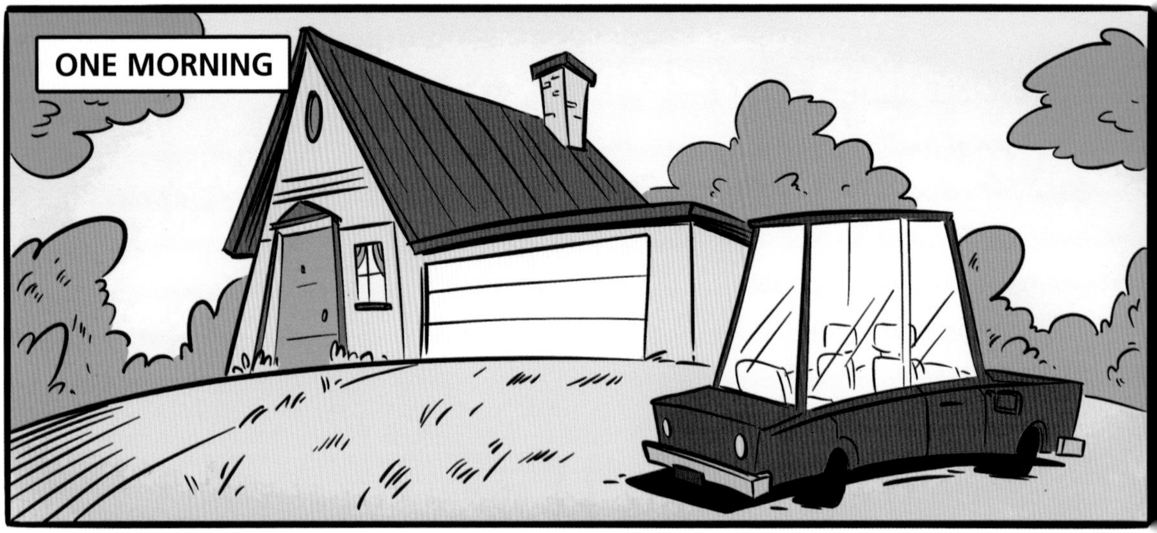
ONE MORNING

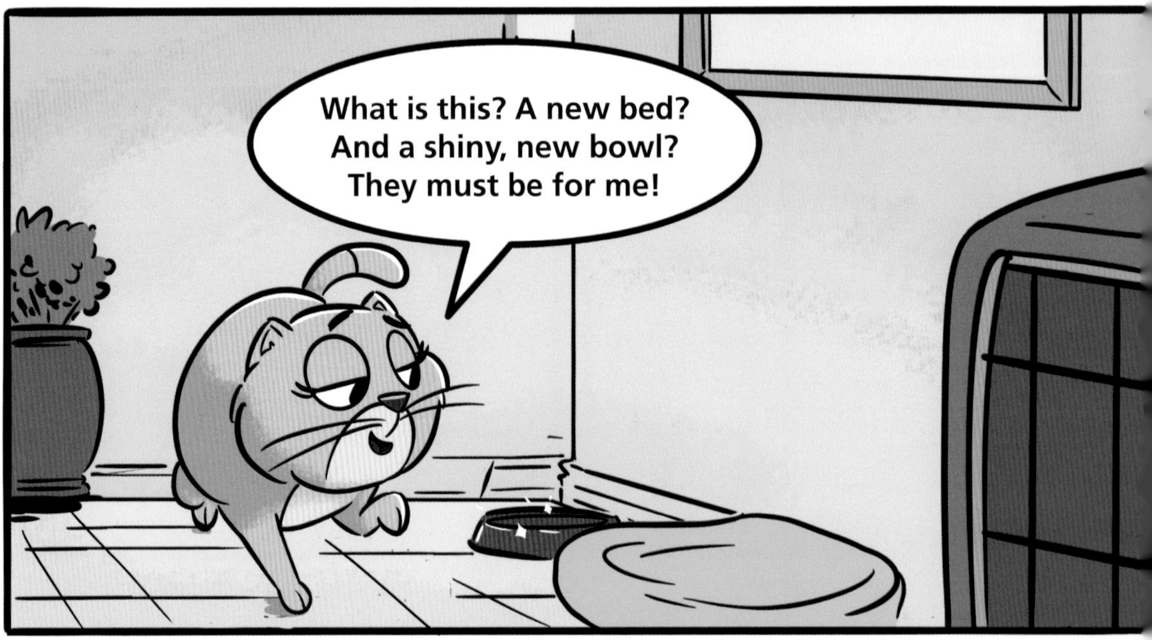
What is this? A new bed?
And a shiny, new bowl?
They must be for me!

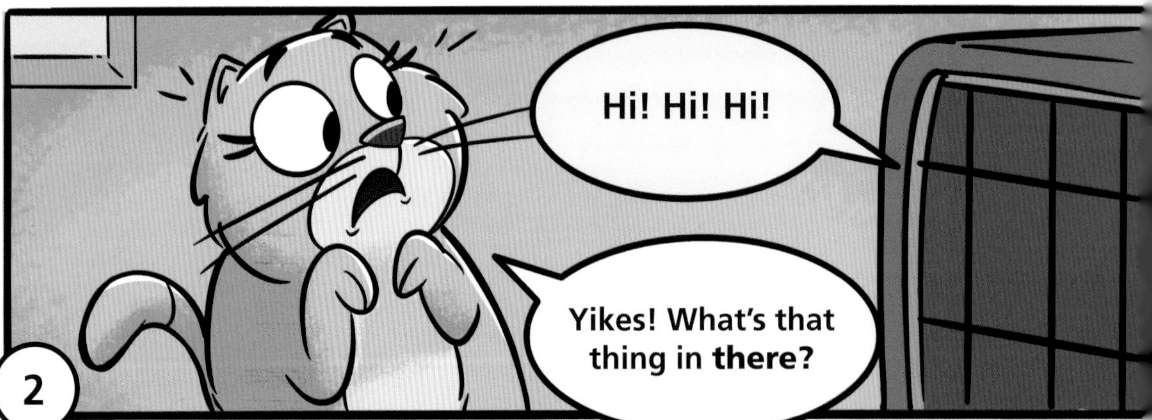
Hi! Hi! Hi!
Yikes! What's that thing in **there**?

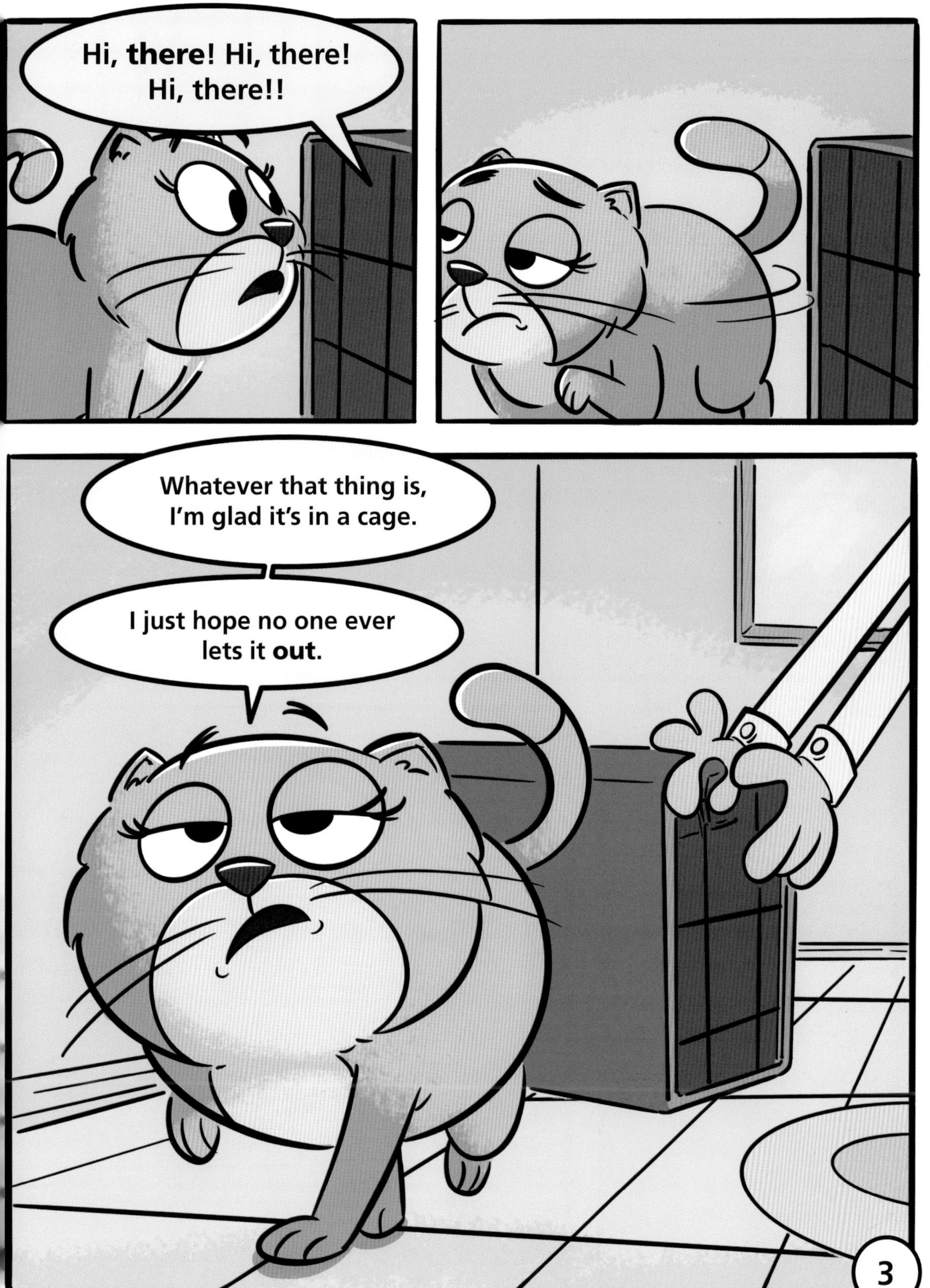

Hi, **there**! Hi, there! Hi, there!!
Whatever that thing is, I'm glad it's in a cage.
I just hope no one ever lets it **out**.

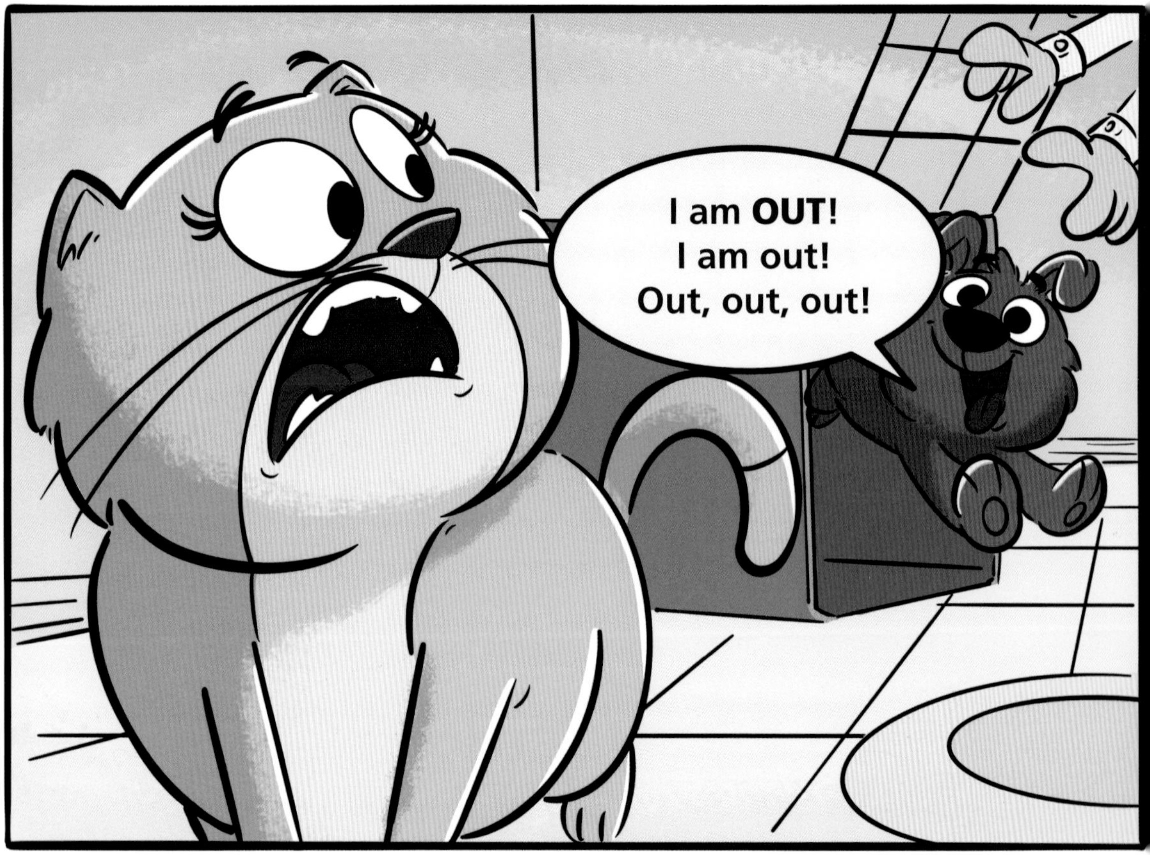
I am **OUT**!
I am out!
Out, out, out!

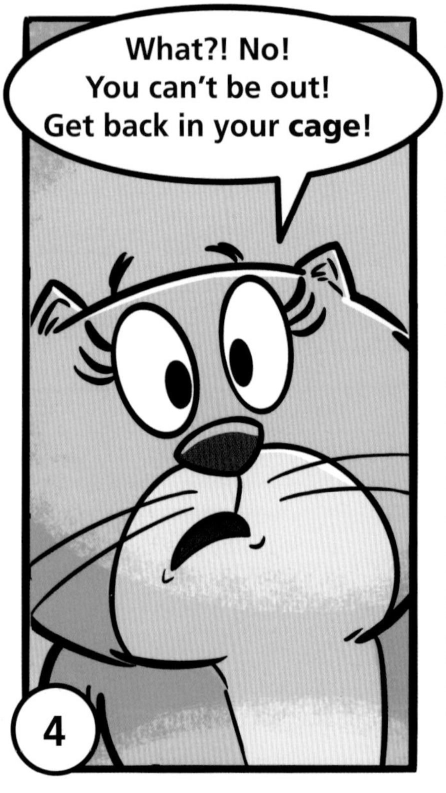
What?! No!
You can't be out!
Get back in your **cage**!

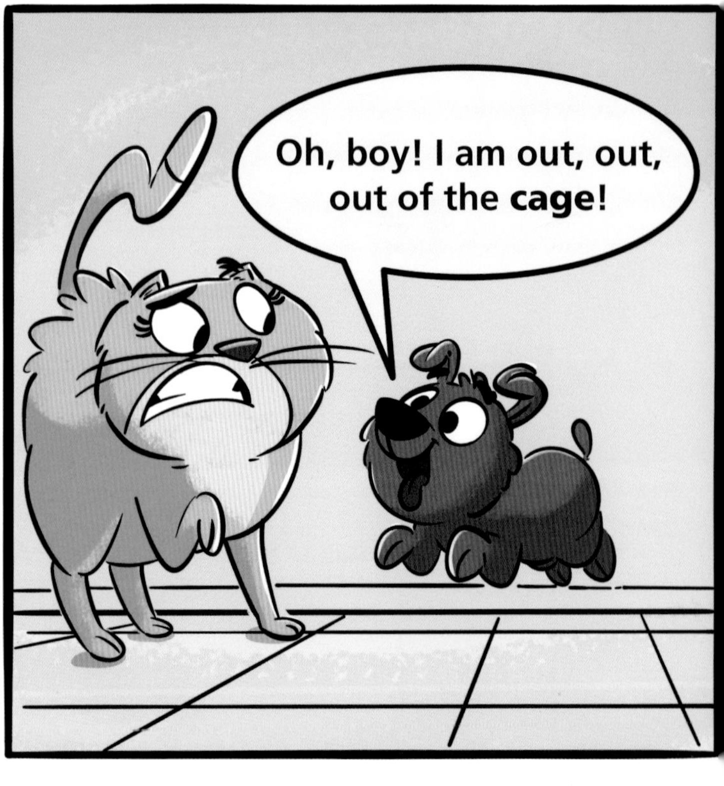
Oh, boy! I am out, out,
out of the **cage**!

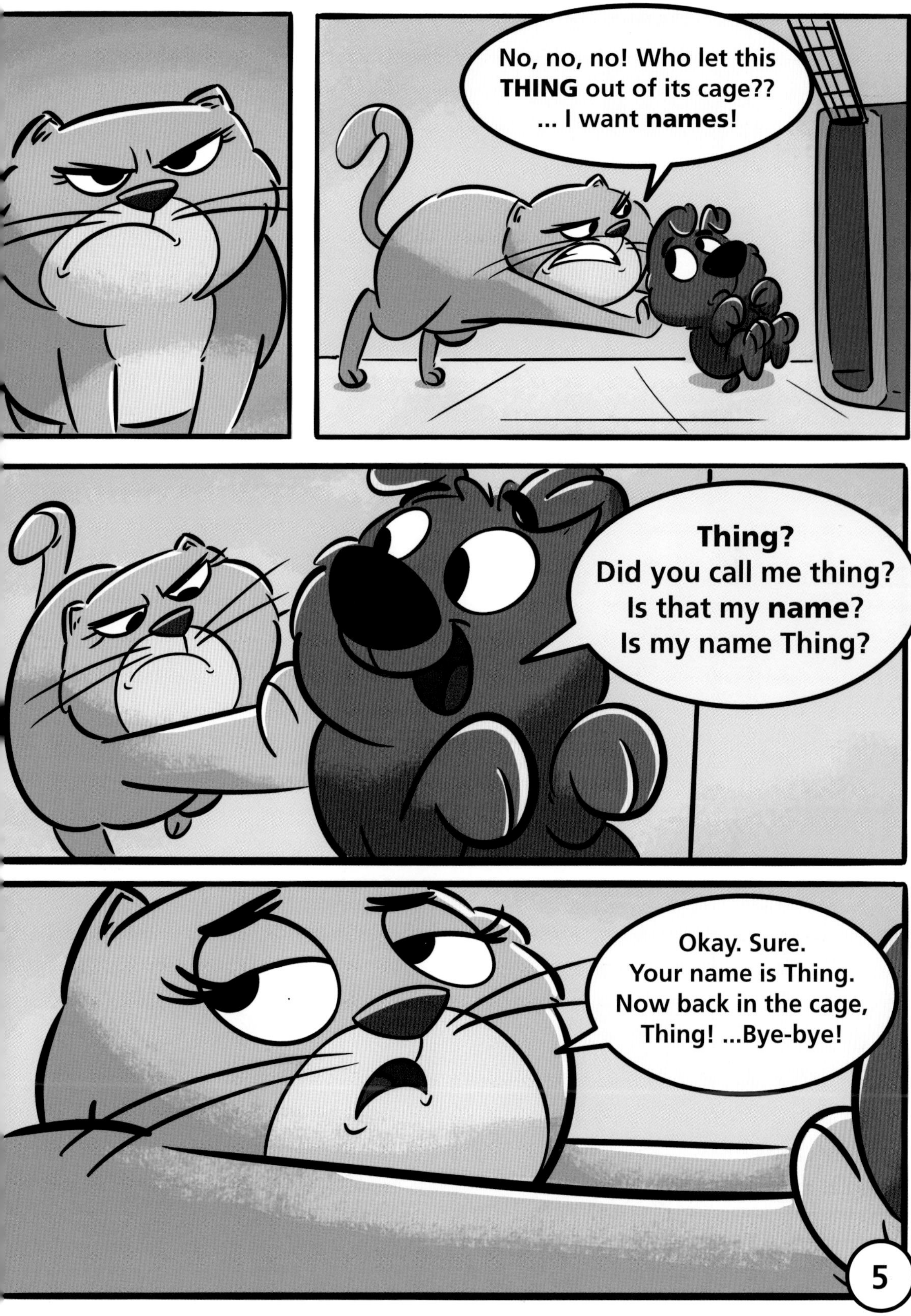
No, no, no! Who let this THING out of its cage?? ... I want names!
Thing? Did you call me thing? Is that my name? Is my name Thing?
Okay. Sure. Your name is Thing. Now back in the cage, Thing! ...Bye-bye!

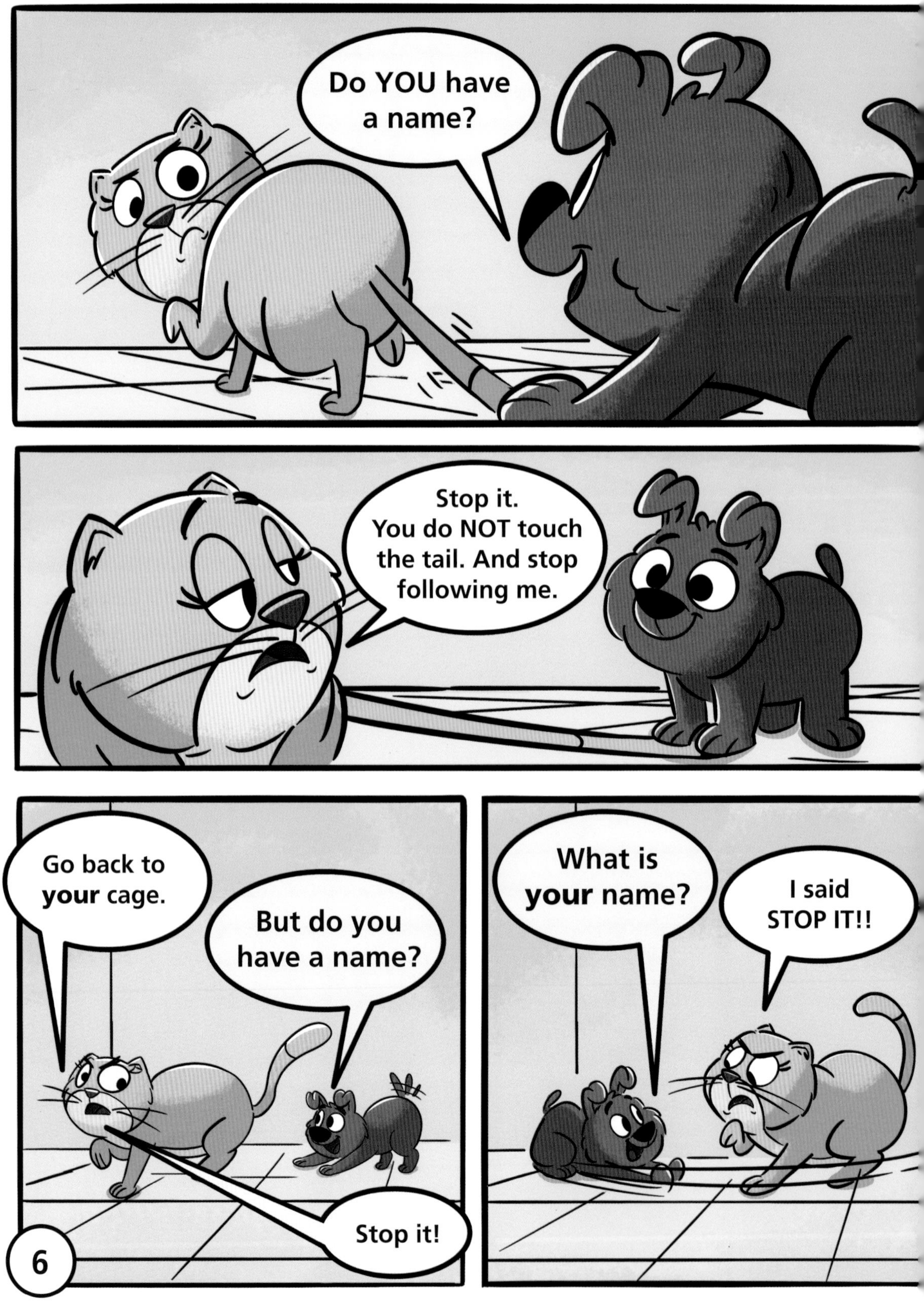
Do YOU have a name?
Stop it. You do NOT touch the tail. And stop following me.
Go back to **your** cage.
But do you have a name?
Stop it!
What is **your** name?
I said STOP IT!!

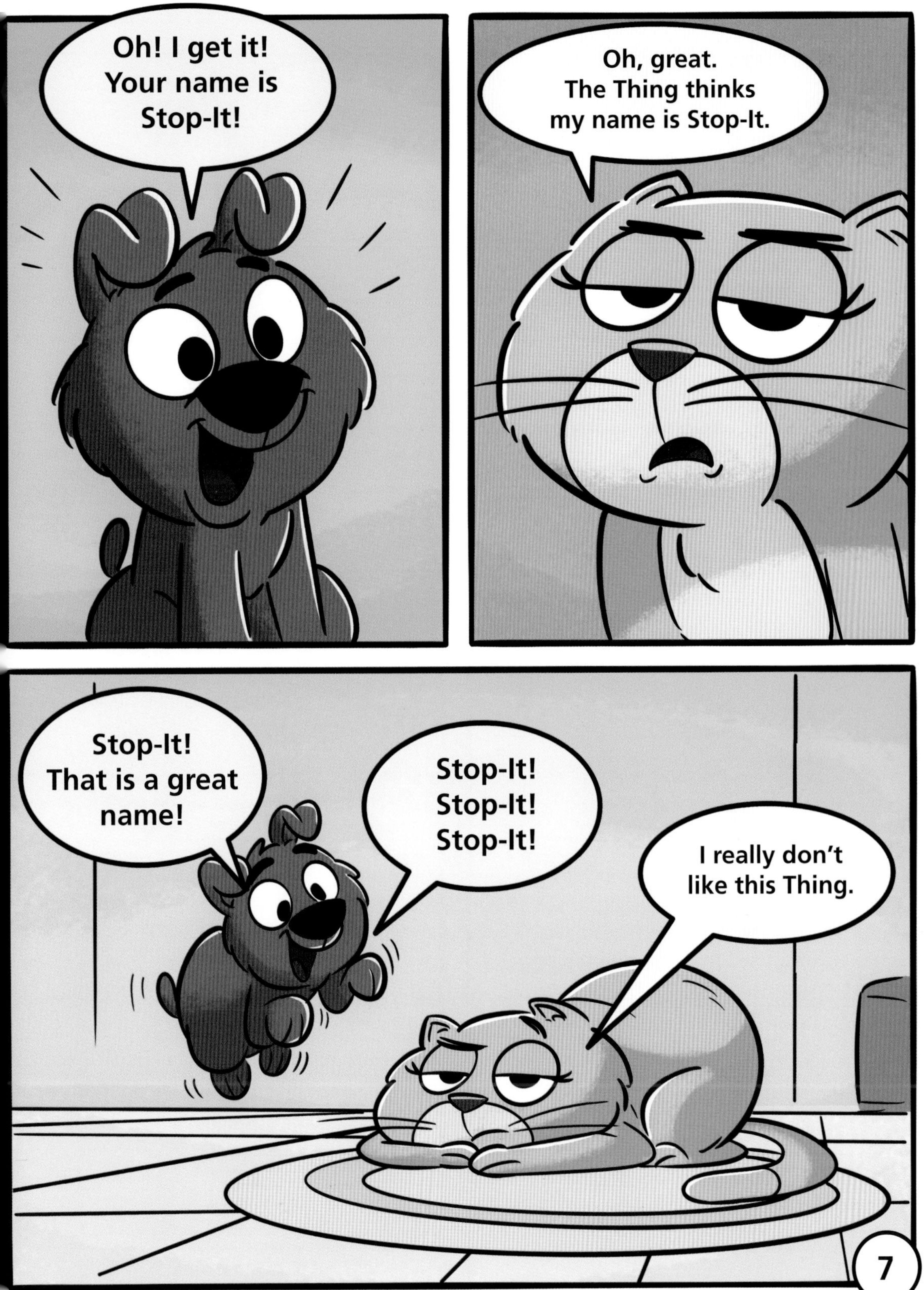
Oh! I get it! Your name is Stop-It!
Oh, great. The Thing thinks my name is Stop-It.
Stop-It! That is a great name!
Stop-It! Stop-It! Stop-It!
I really don't like this Thing.

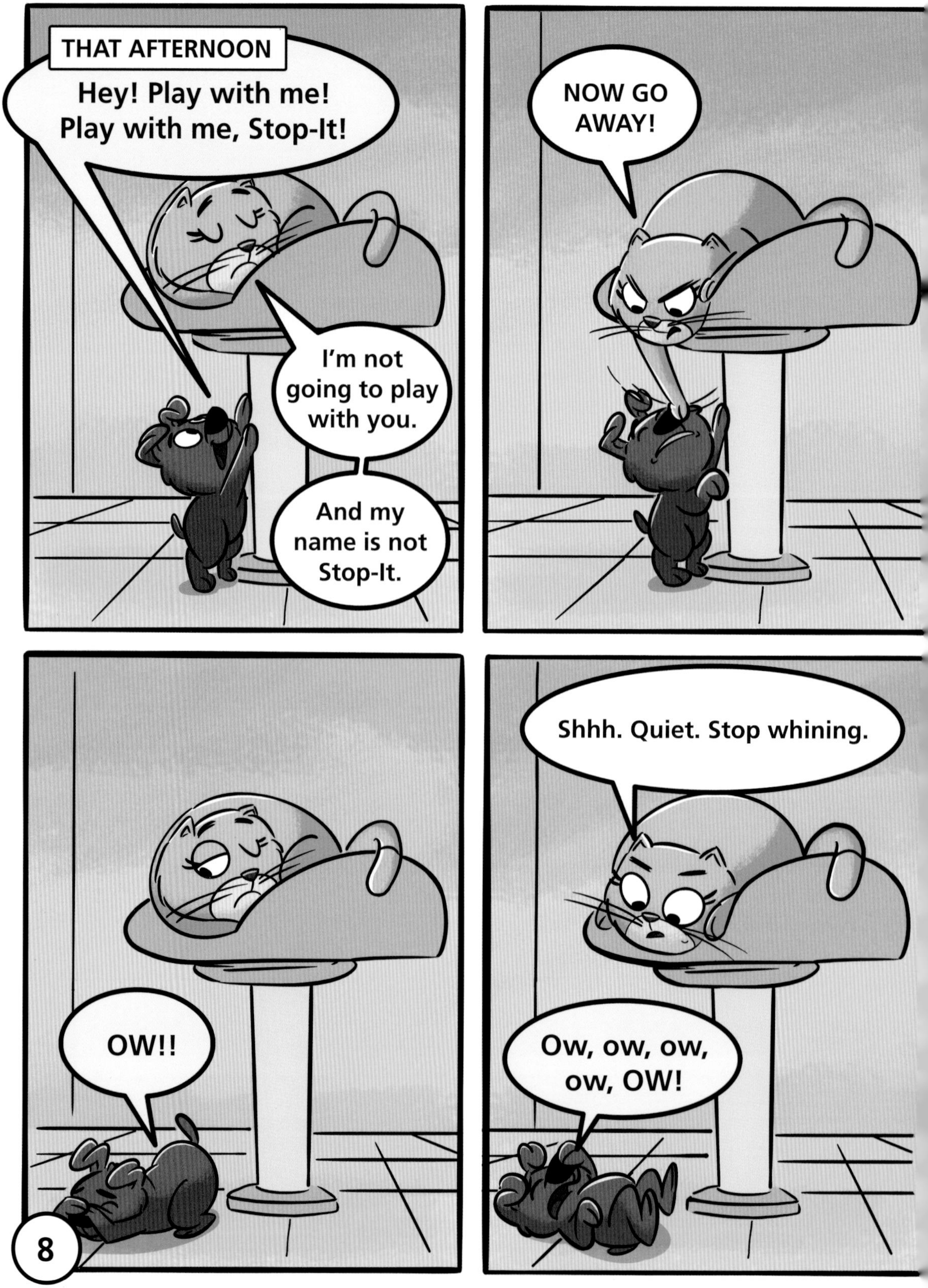
THAT AFTERNOON
Hey! Play with me! Play with me, Stop-It!
I'm not going to play with you.
And my name is not Stop-It.
NOW GO AWAY!
OW!!
Shhh. Quiet. Stop whining.
Ow, ow, ow, ow, OW!

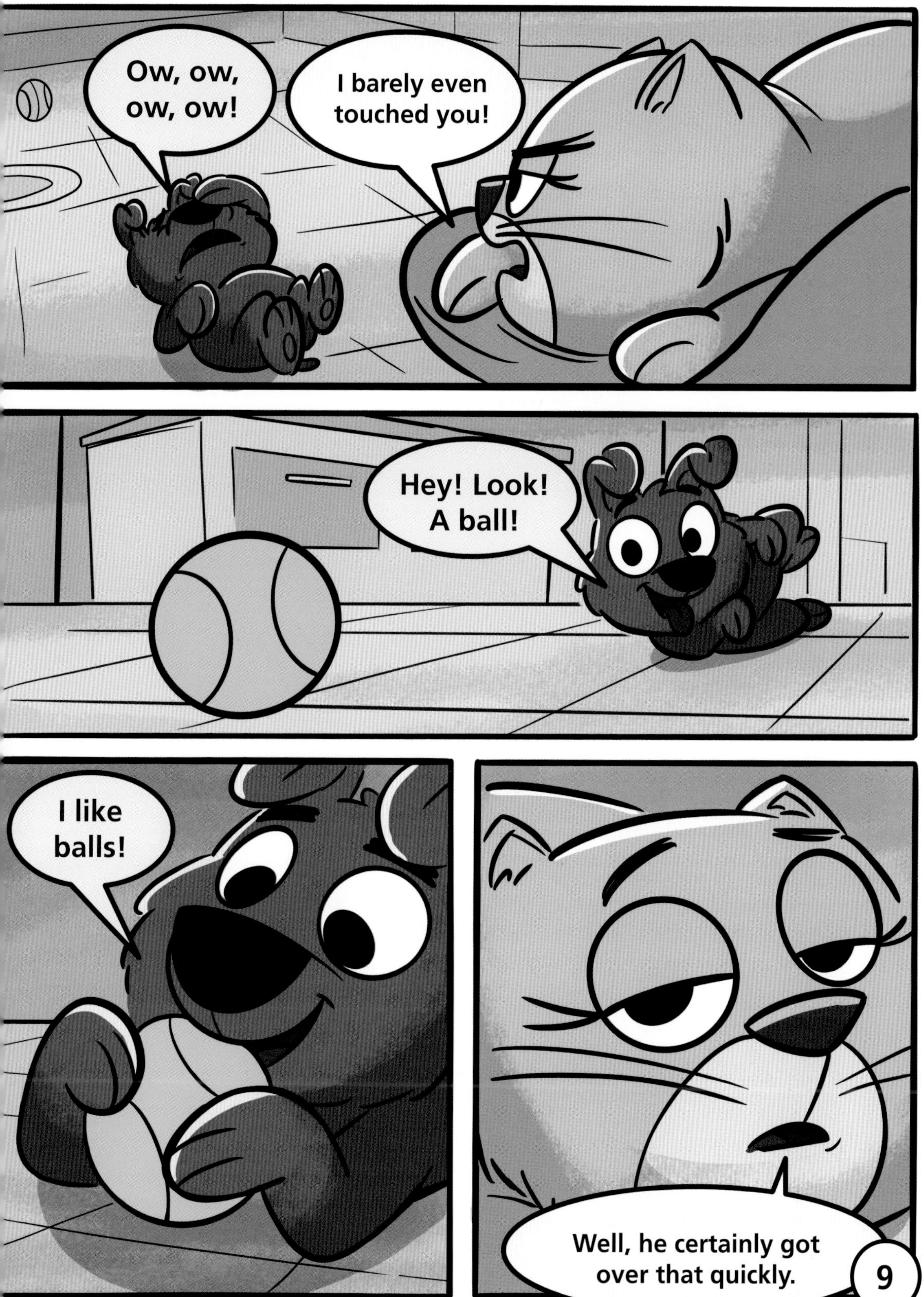
Ow, ow, ow, ow!
I barely even touched you!
Hey! Look! A ball!
I like balls!
Well, he certainly got over that quickly.

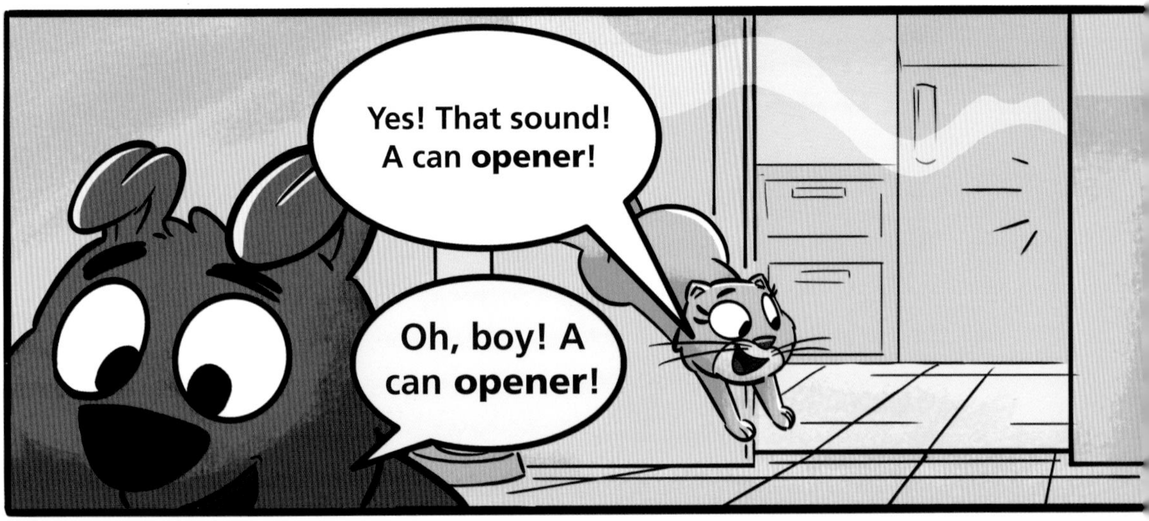
Yes! That sound! A can **opener**!
Oh, boy! A can **opener**!

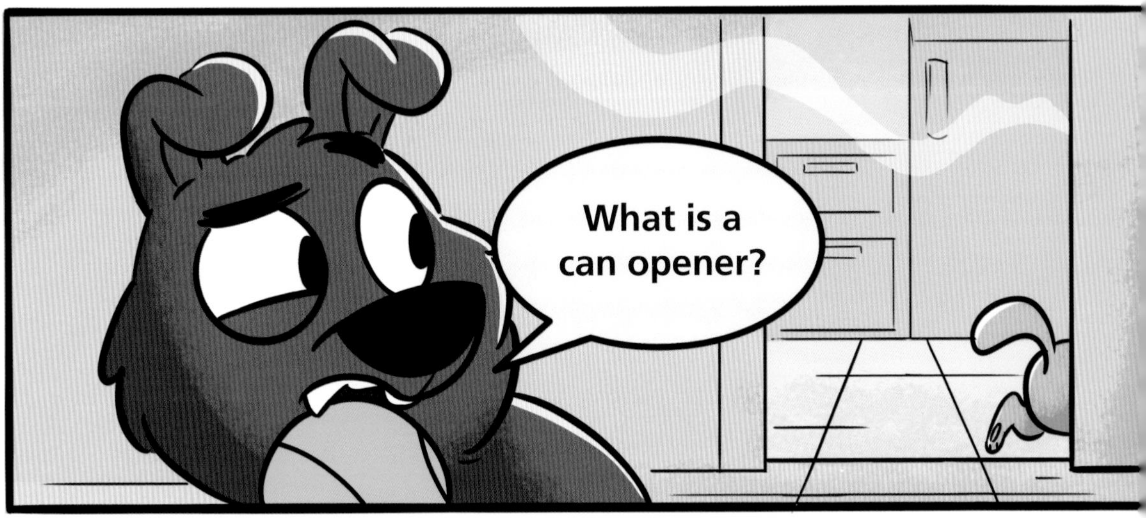
What is a can opener?

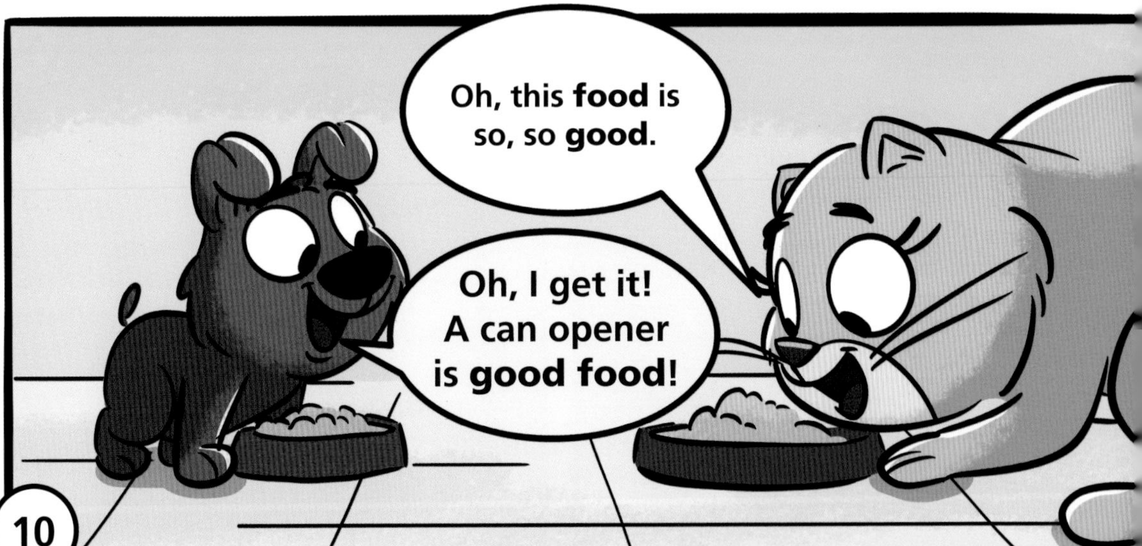
Oh, this **food** is so, so **good**.
Oh, I get it! A can opener is **good food**!

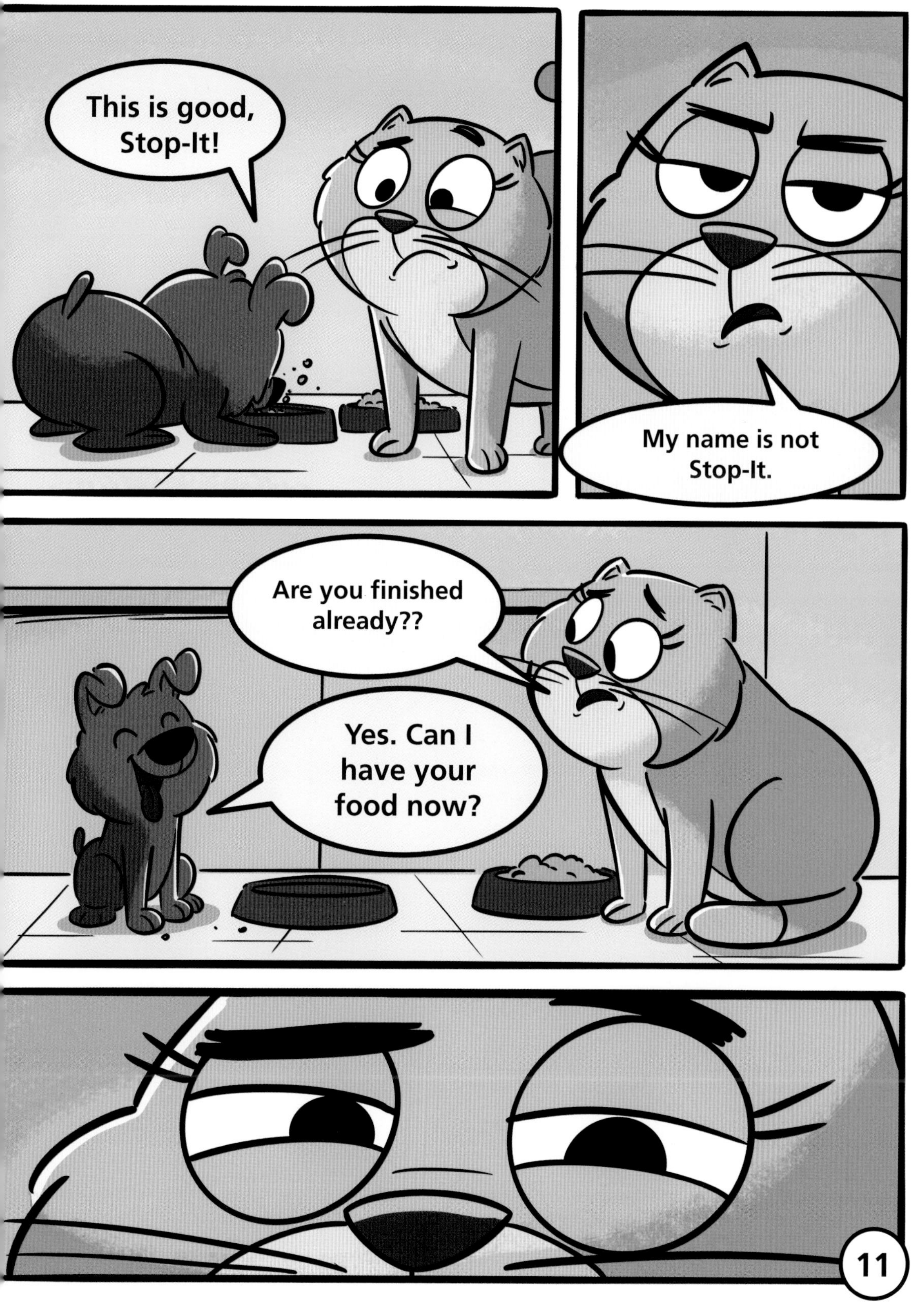
This is good, Stop-It!
My name is not Stop-It.
Are you finished already??
Yes. Can I have your food now?

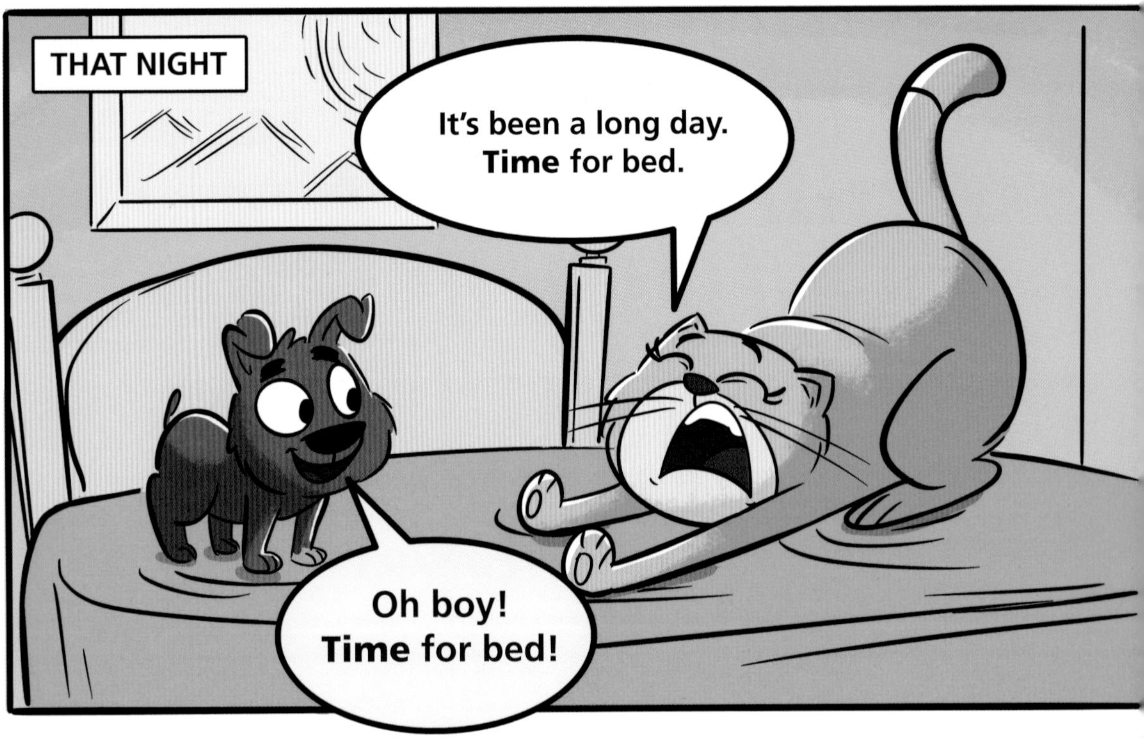
THAT NIGHT
It's been a long day. **Time** for bed.
Oh boy! **Time** for bed!

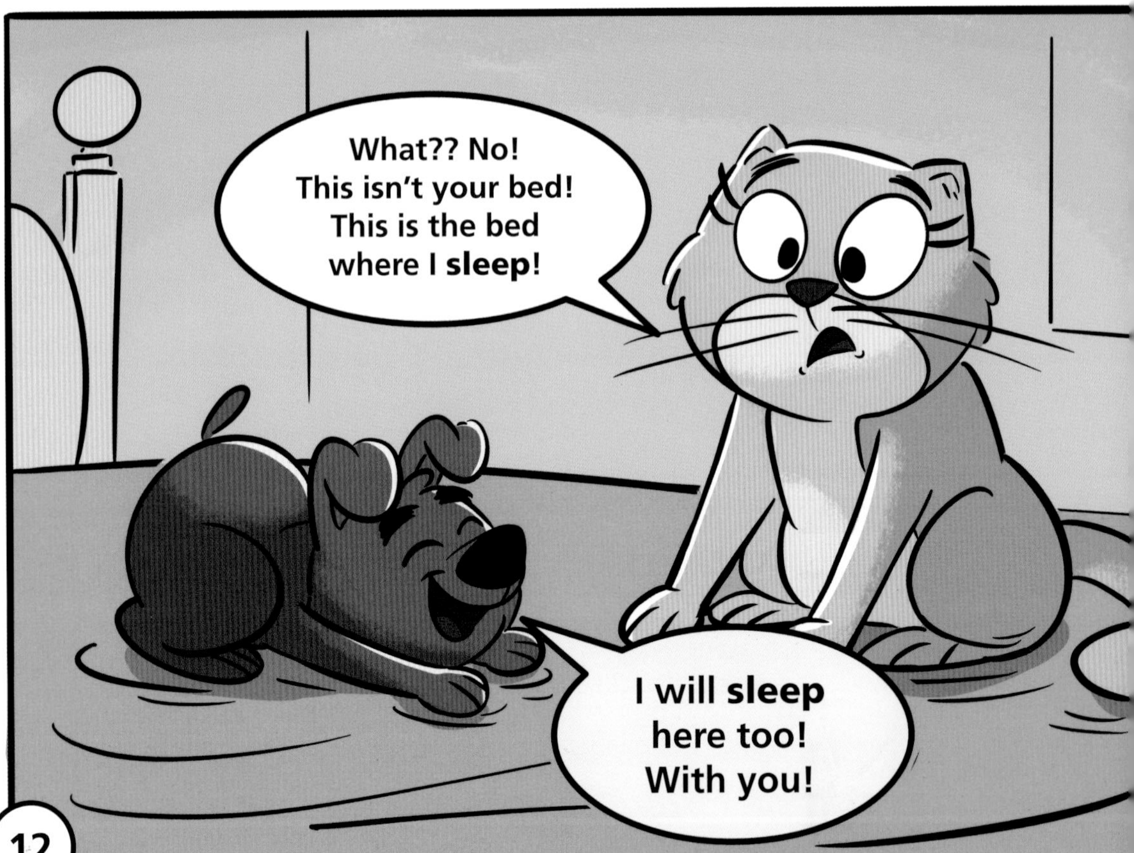
What?? No! This isn't your bed! This is the bed where I **sleep**!
I will **sleep** here too! With you!

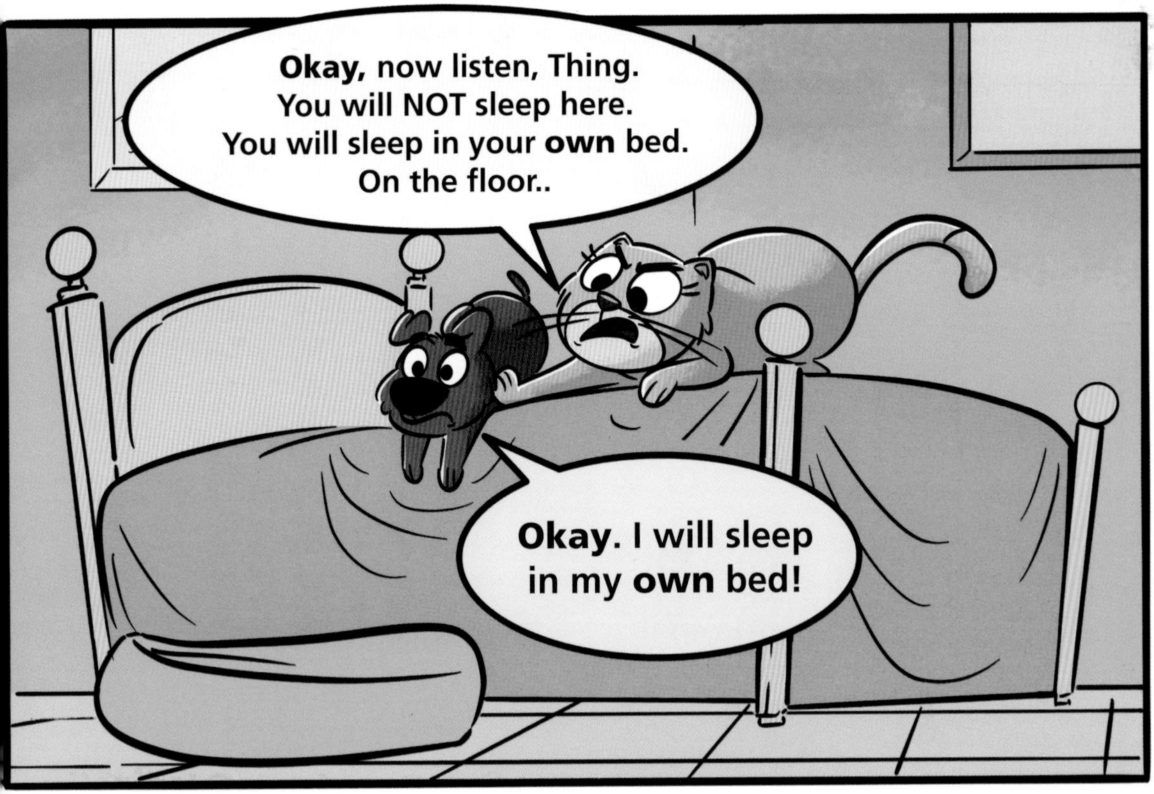
Okay, now listen, Thing.
You will NOT sleep here.
You will sleep in your **own** bed.
On the floor..
Okay. I will sleep in my **own** bed!

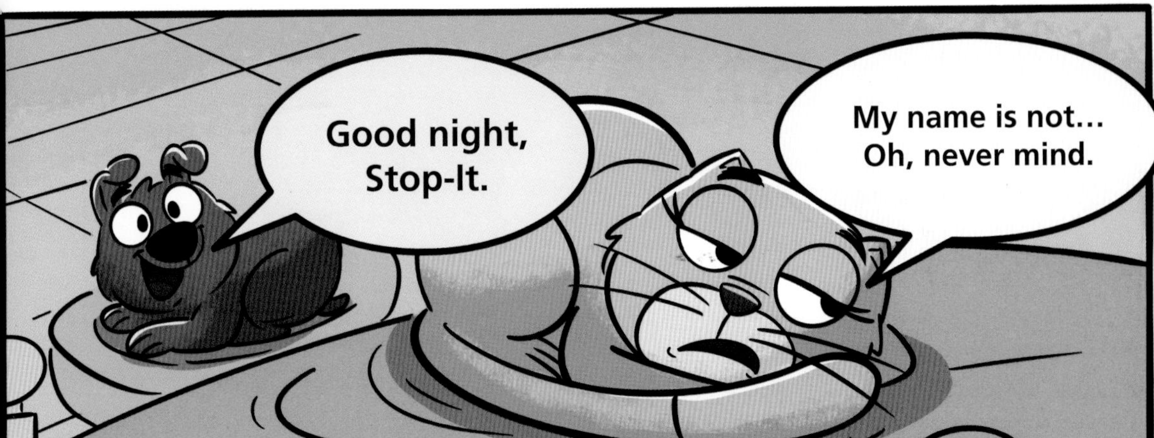
Good night, Stop-It.
My name is not… Oh, never mind.

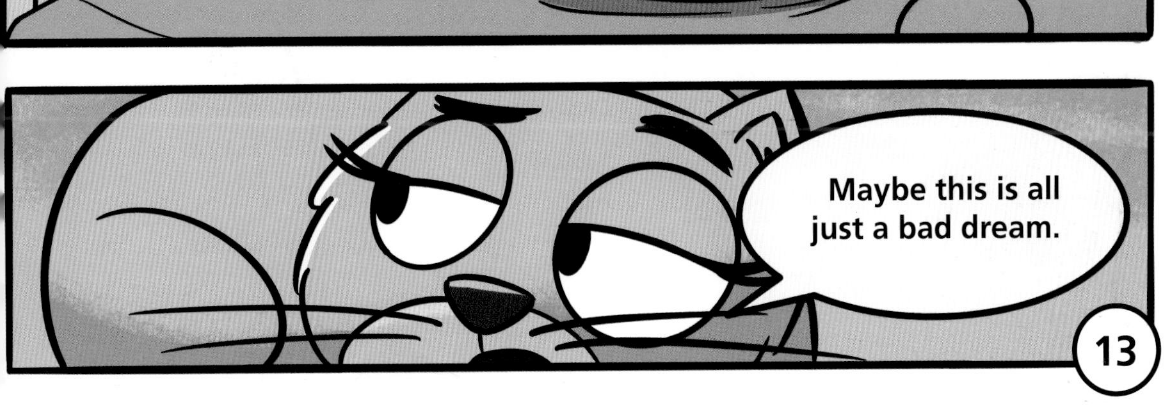
Maybe this is all just a bad dream.

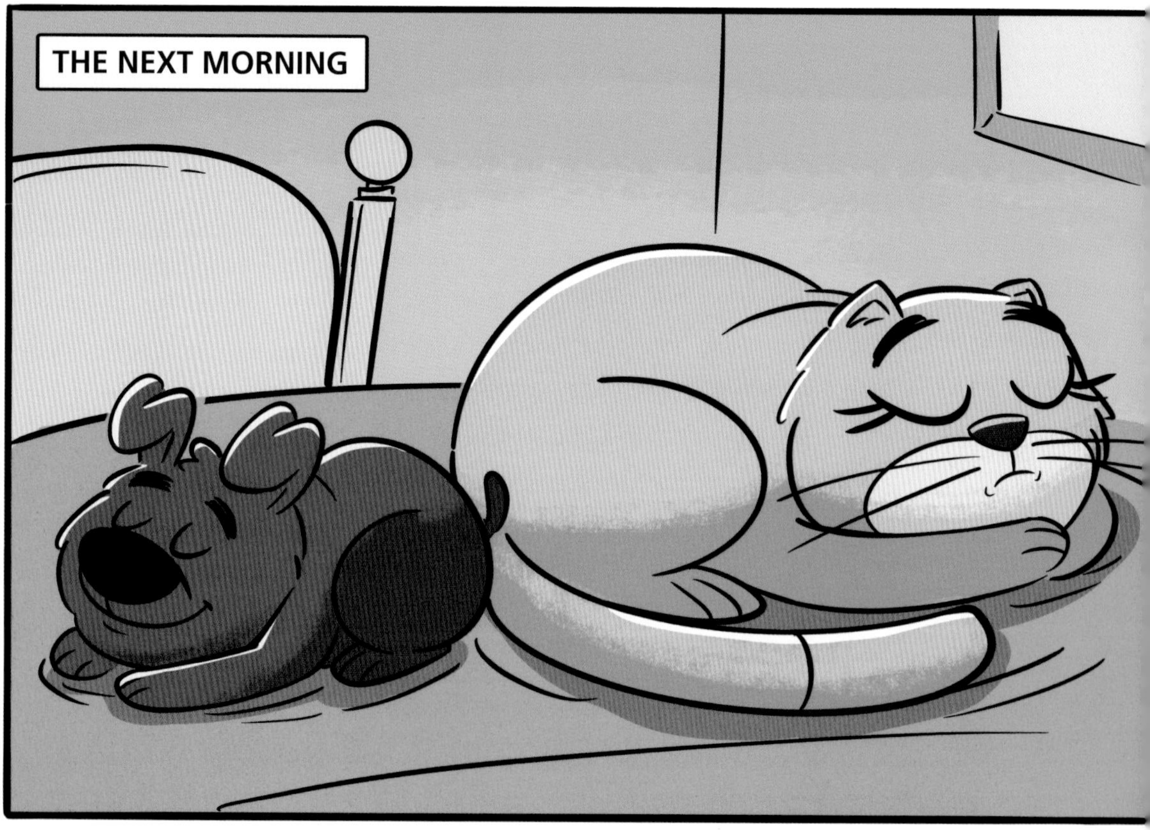
THE NEXT MORNING

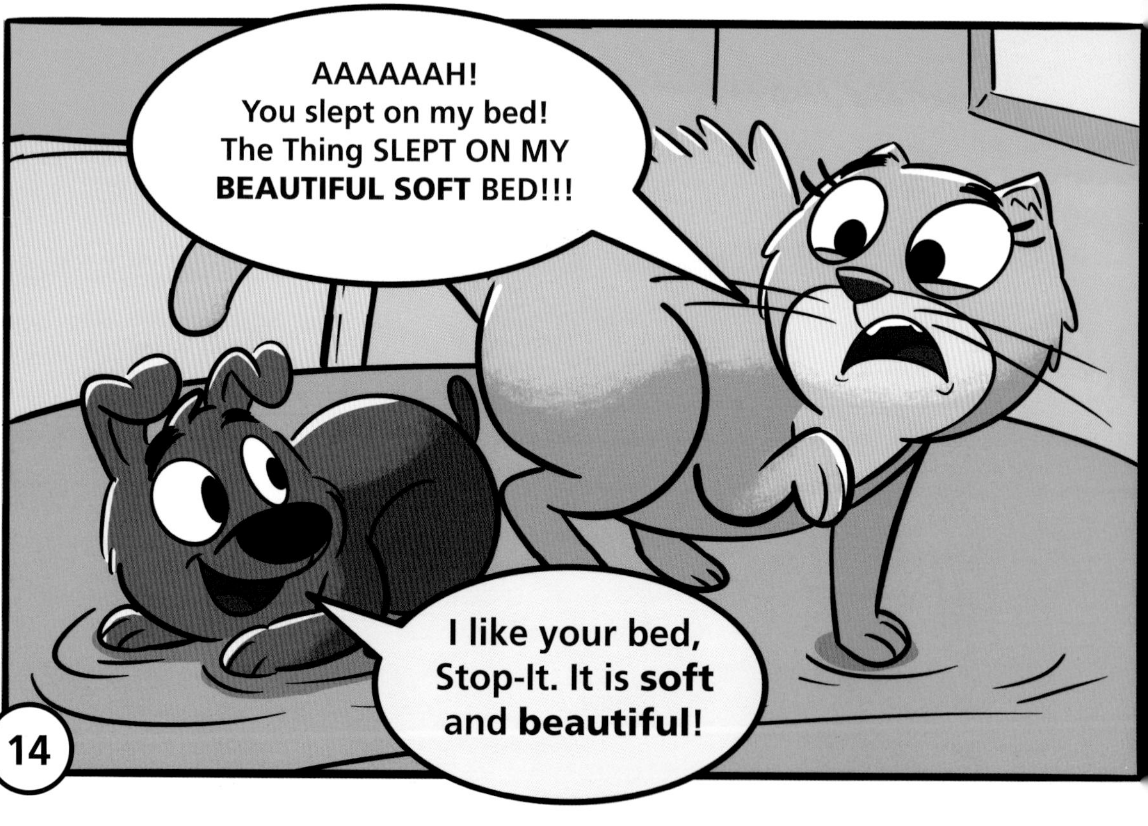
AAAAAAH!
You slept on my bed!
The Thing SLEPT ON MY
BEAUTIFUL SOFT BED!!!
I like your bed,
Stop-It. It is **soft**
and **beautiful**!

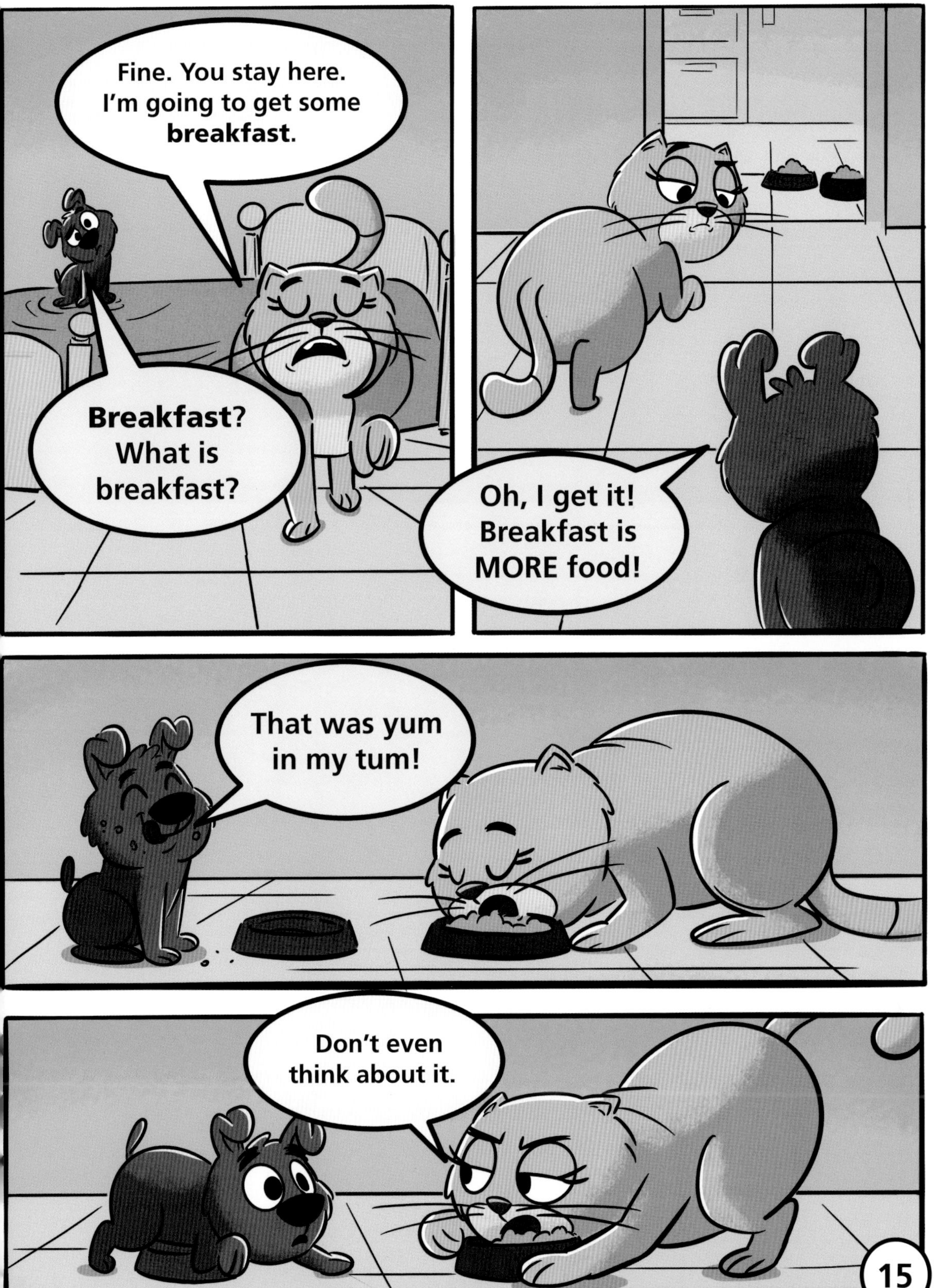
Fine. You stay here. I'm going to get some **breakfast**.
Breakfast? What is breakfast?
Oh, I get it! Breakfast is MORE food!
That was yum in my tum!
Don't even think about it.

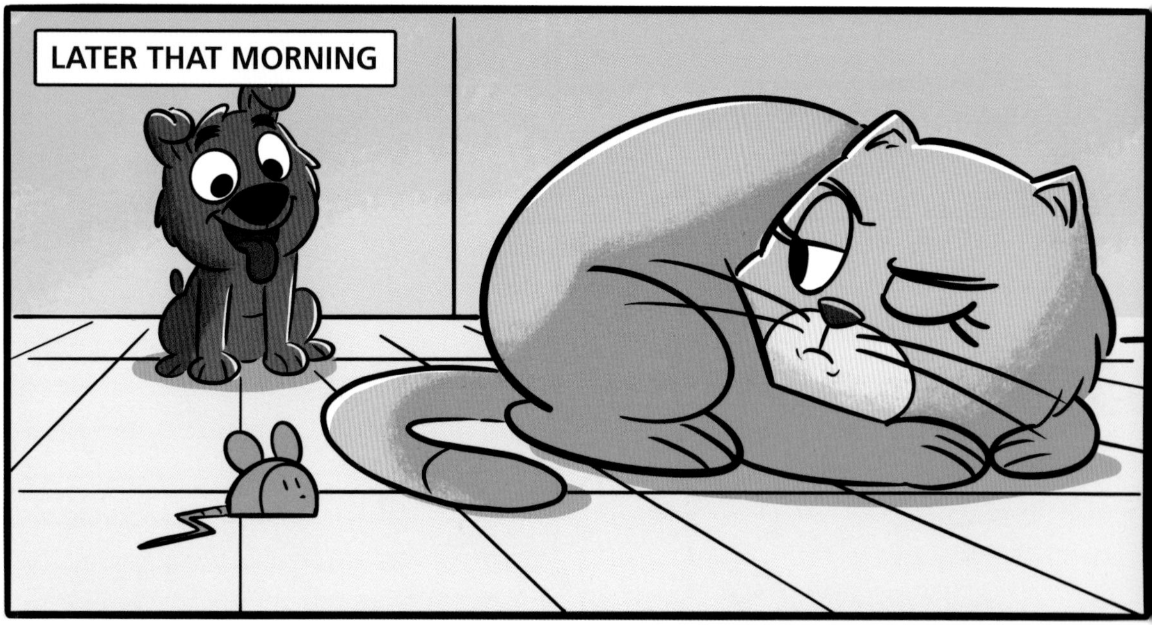
LATER THAT MORNING

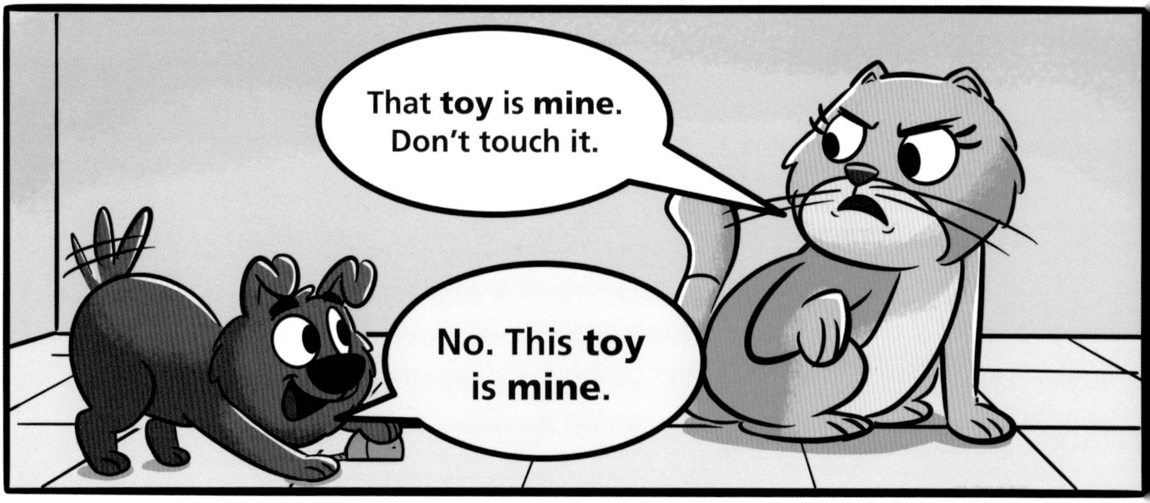
That **toy** is **mine**. Don't touch it.
No. This **toy** is **mine.**

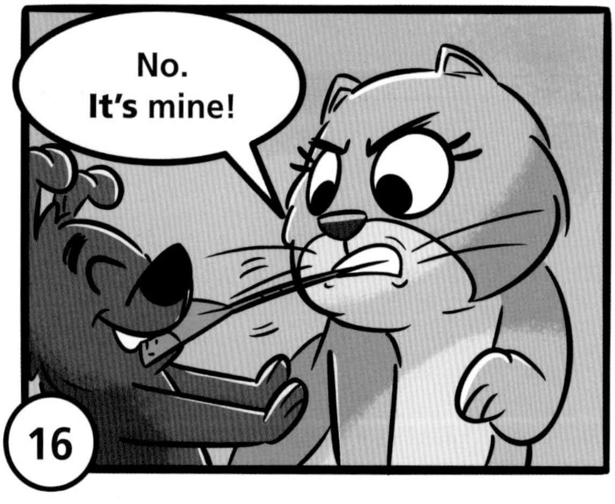
No. **It's** mine!

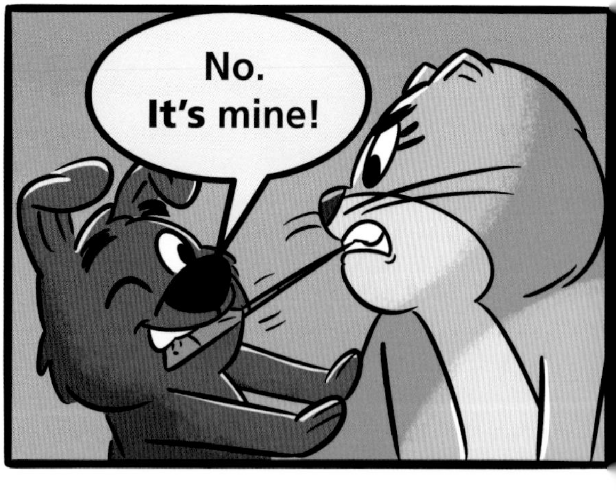
No. **It's** mine!

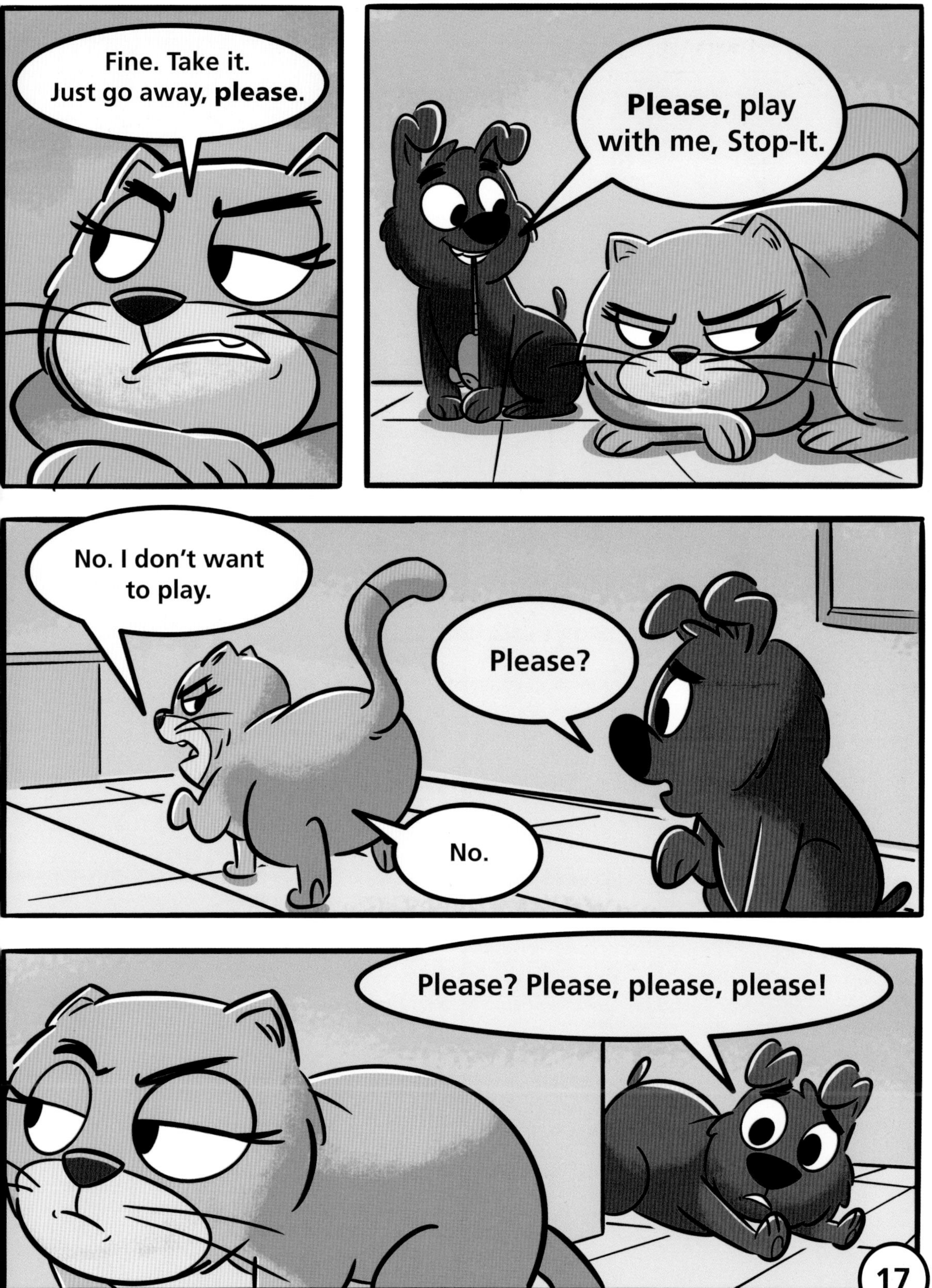
Fine. Take it.
Just go away, **please.**
Please, play with me, Stop-It.
No. I don't want to play.
Please?
No.
Please? Please, please, please!

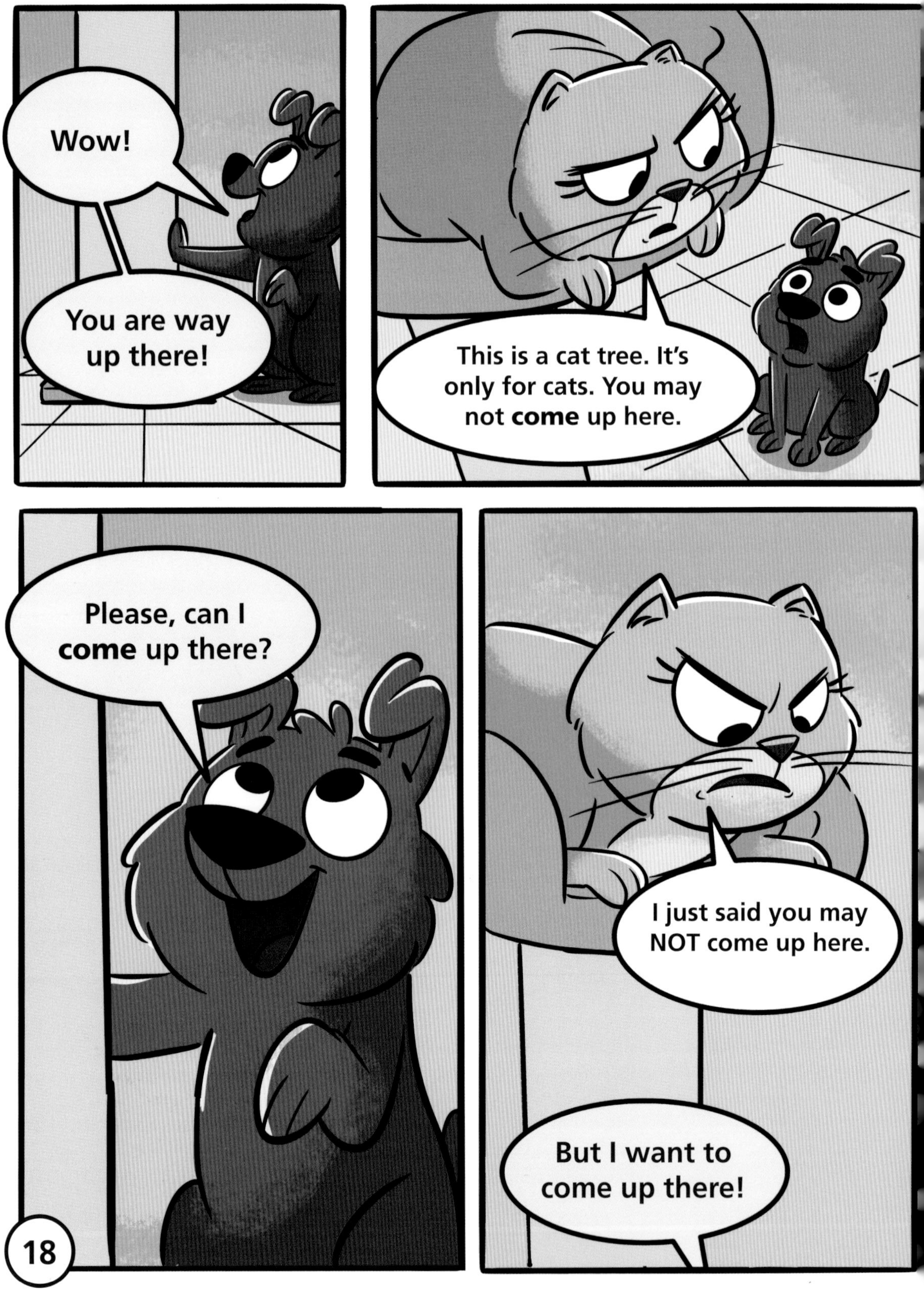
Wow!
You are way up there!
This is a cat tree. It's only for cats. You may not **come** up here.
Please, can I **come** up there?
I just said you may NOT come up here.
But I want to come up there!

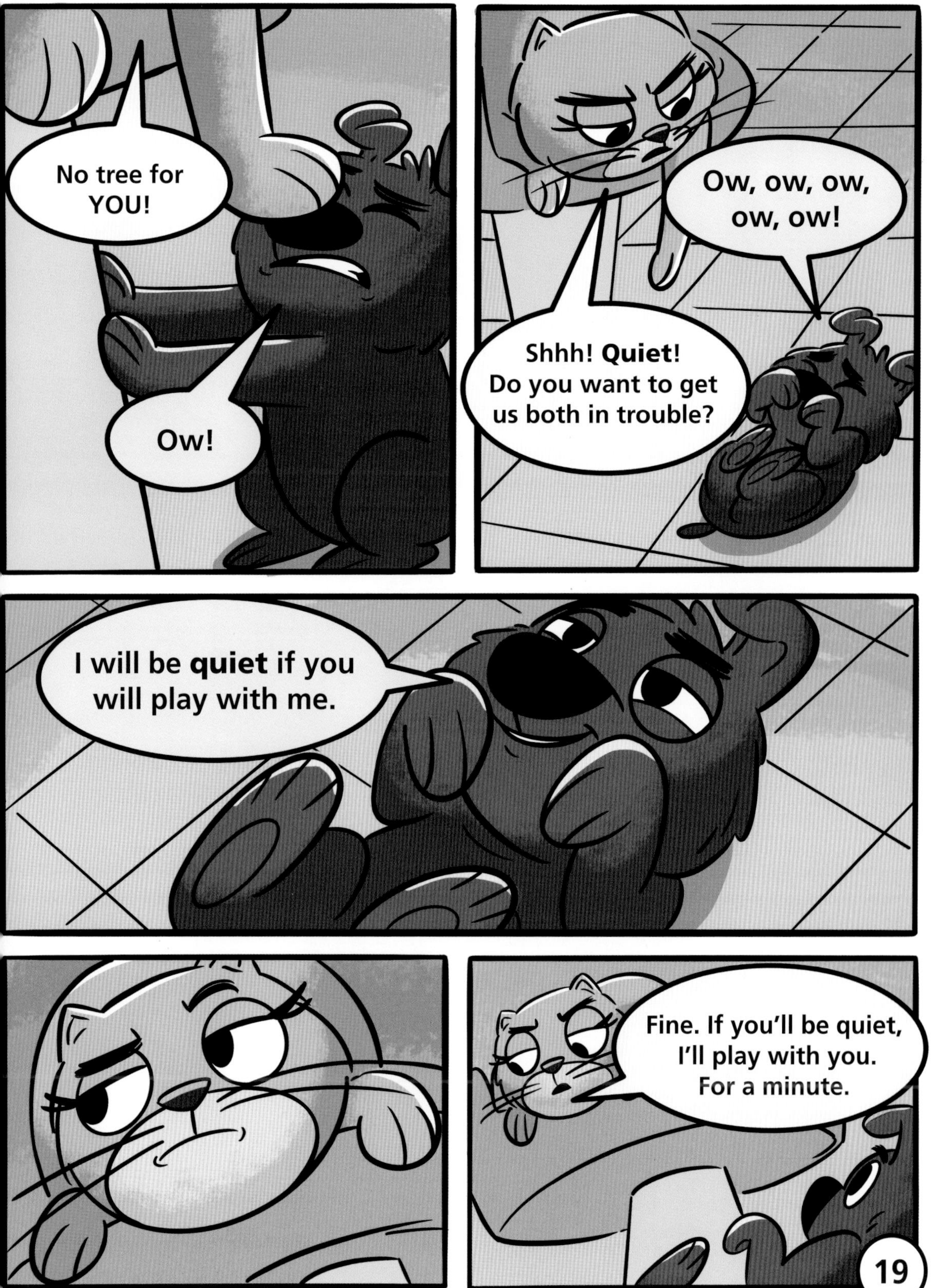
No tree for YOU!
Ow!
Ow, ow, ow, ow, ow!
Shhh! **Quiet**! Do you want to get us both in trouble?
I will be **quiet** if you will play with me.
Fine. If you'll be quiet, I'll play with you. For a minute.

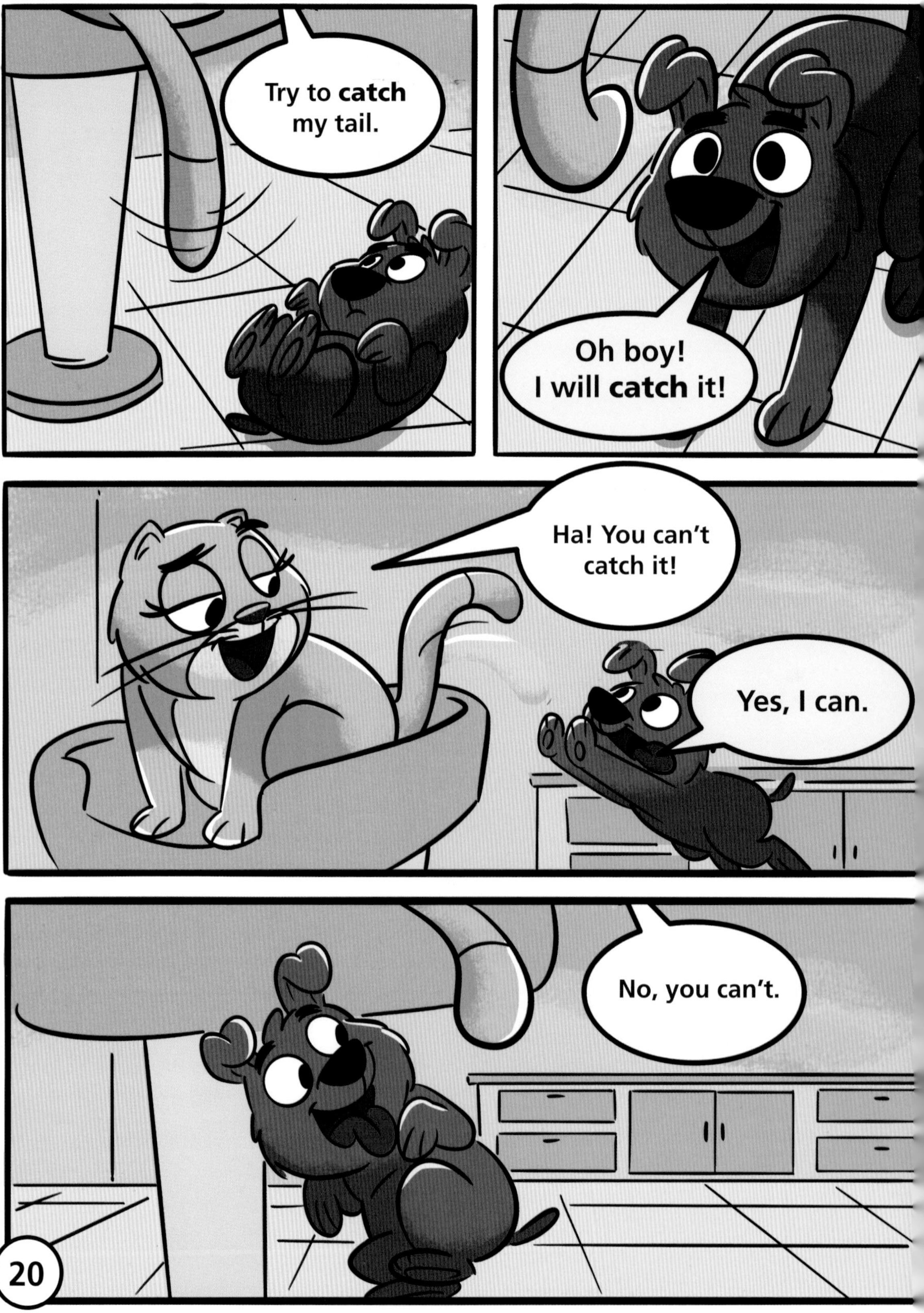
Try to **catch** my tail.
Oh boy! I will **catch** it!
Ha! You can't catch it!
Yes, I can.
No, you can't.

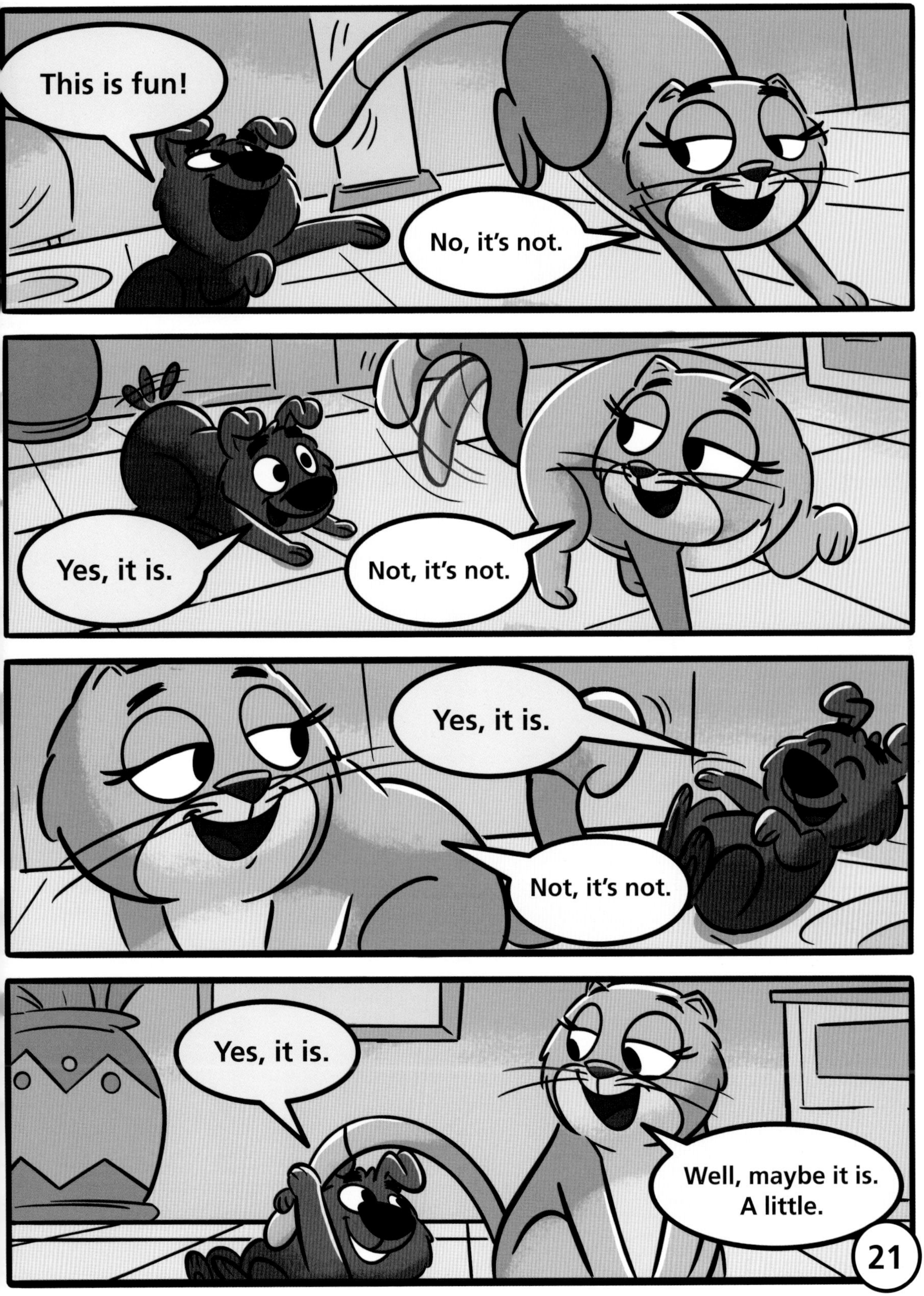
This is fun!
No, it’s not.
Yes, it is.
Not, it’s not.
Yes, it is.
Not, it’s not.
Yes, it is.
Well, maybe it is. A little.

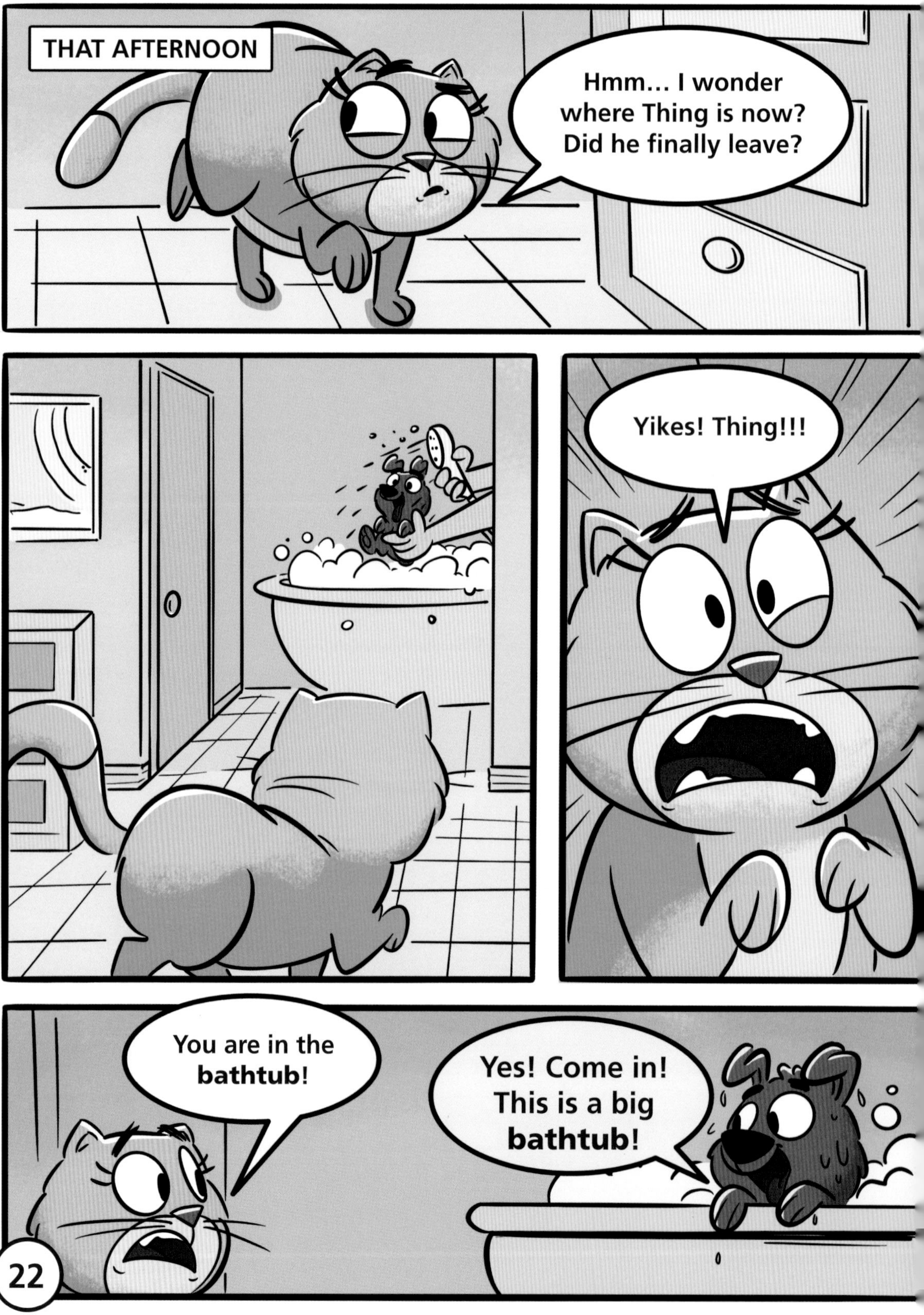
THAT AFTERNOON
Hmm... I wonder where Thing is now? Did he finally leave?
Yikes! Thing!!!
You are in the **bathtub**!
Yes! Come in! This is a big **bathtub**!

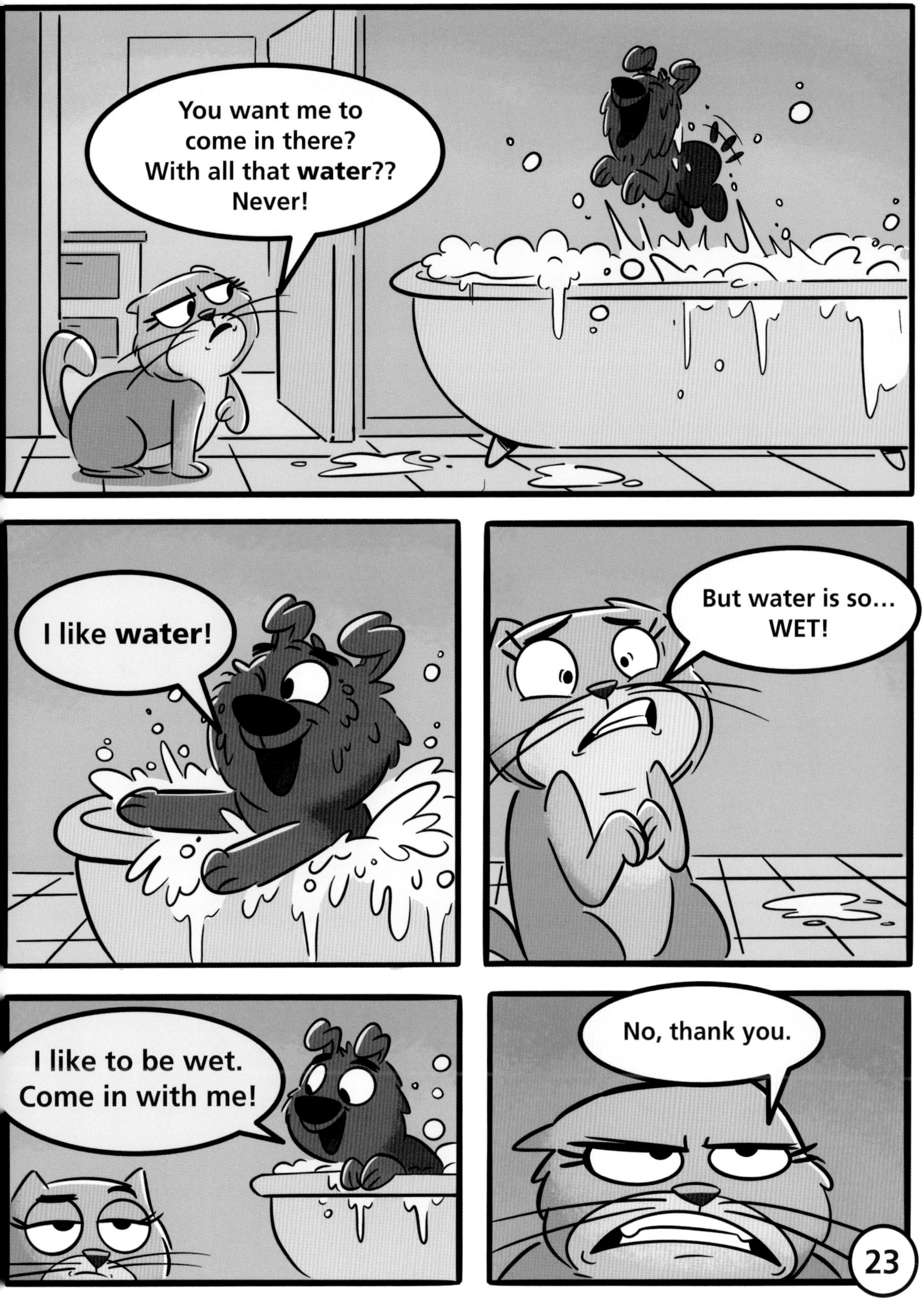
You want me to come in there? With all that **water**?? Never!
I like **water**!
But water is so... WET!
I like to be wet. Come in with me!
No, thank you.

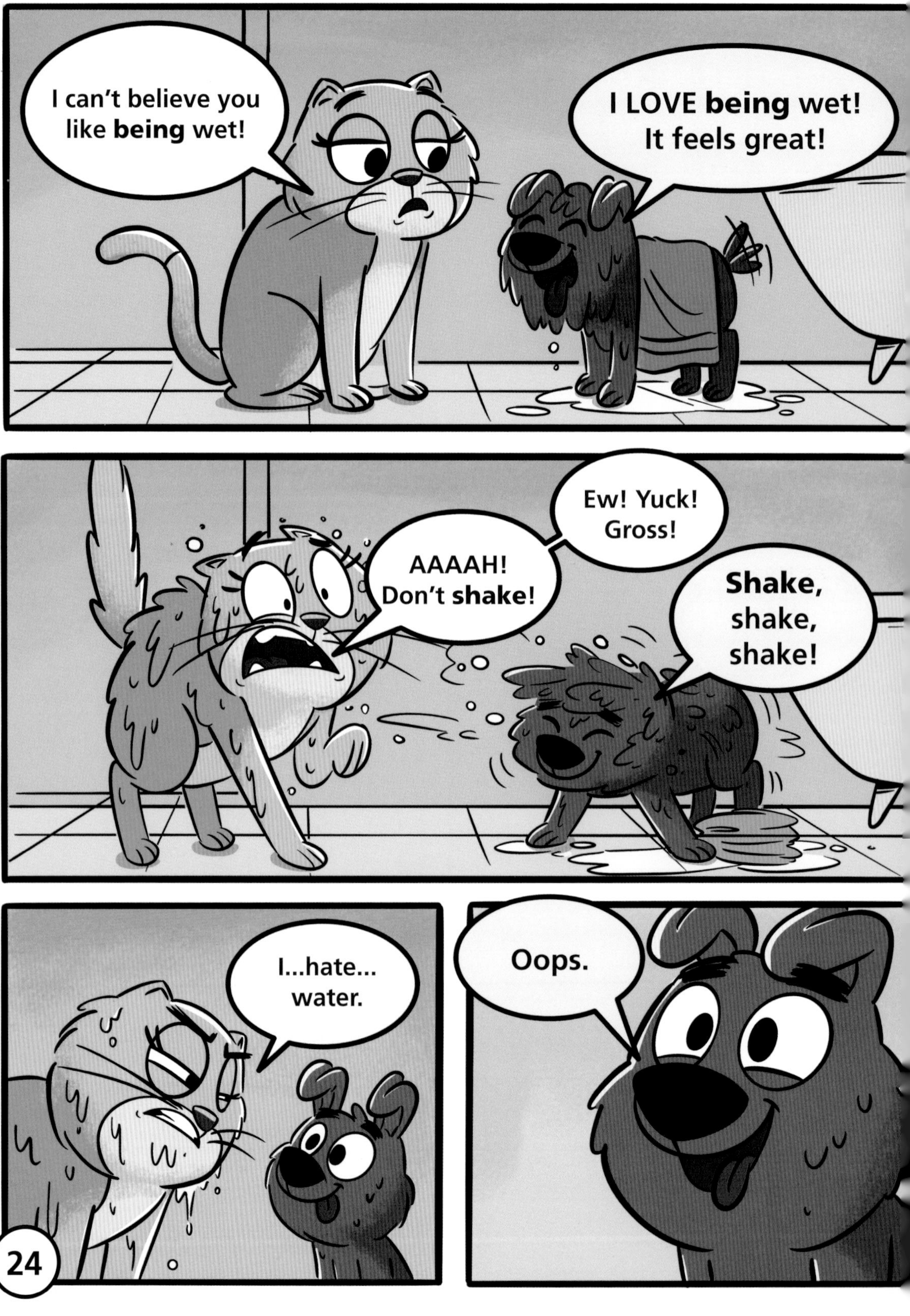
I can't believe you like **being** wet!
I LOVE **being** wet! It feels great!
AAAAH! Don't **shake**!
Ew! Yuck! Gross!
Shake, shake, shake!
I...hate... water.
Oops.

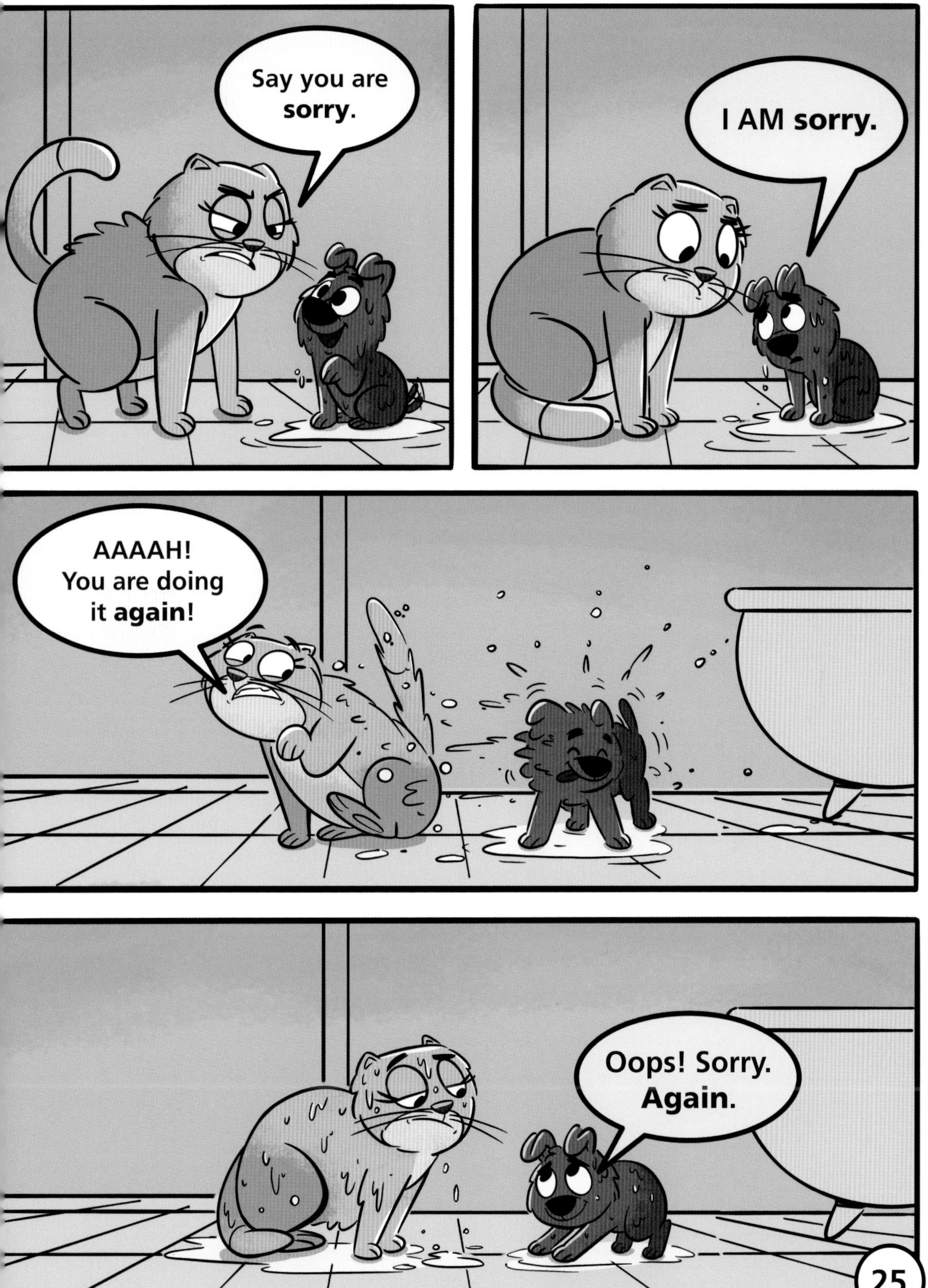
Say you are **sorry**.
I AM **sorry**.
AAAAH! You are doing it **again**!
Oops! Sorry. **Again**.

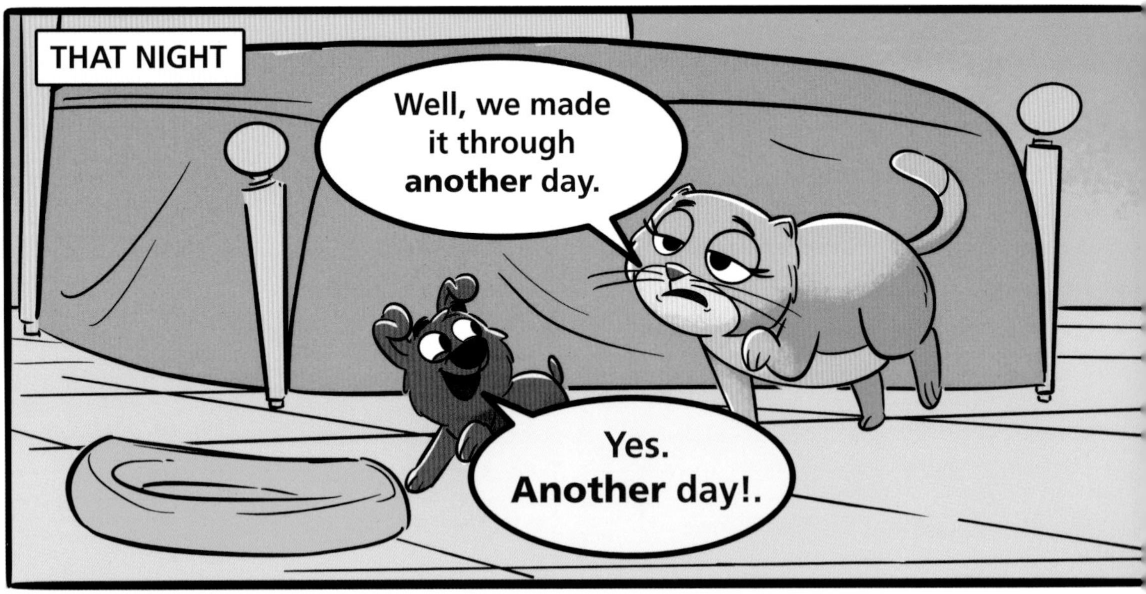
THAT NIGHT
Well, we made it through **another** day.
Yes. **Another** day!.

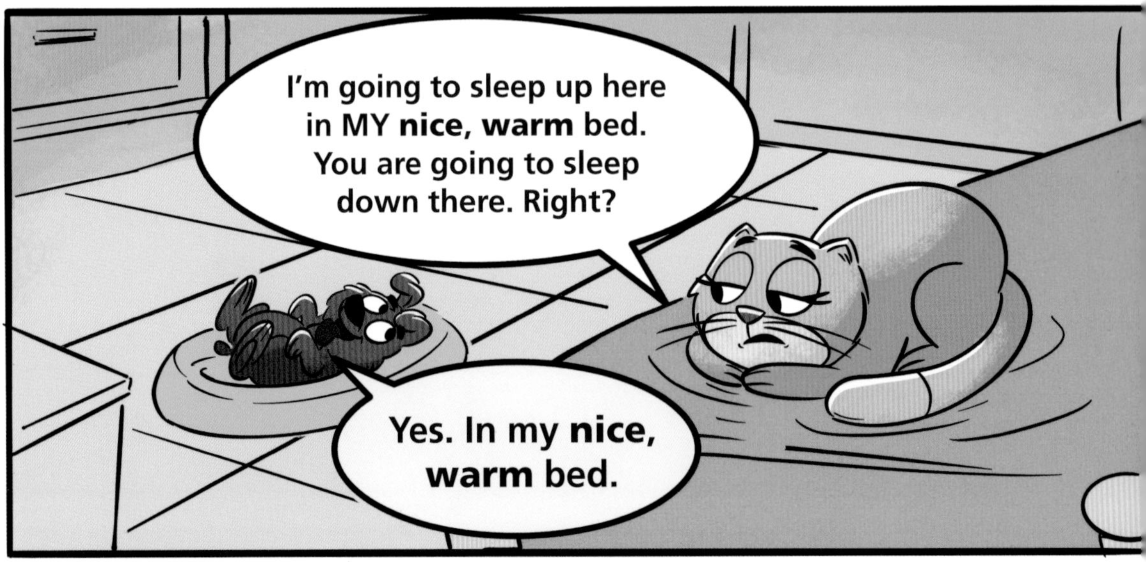
I'm going to sleep up here in MY **nice, warm** bed. You are going to sleep down there. Right?
Yes. In my **nice, warm** bed.

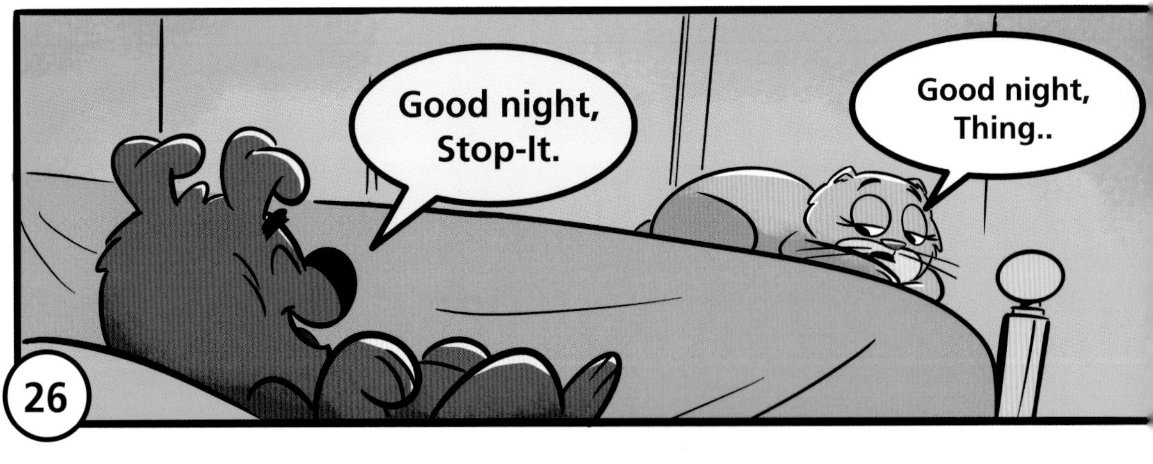
Good night, Stop-It.
Good night, Thing..

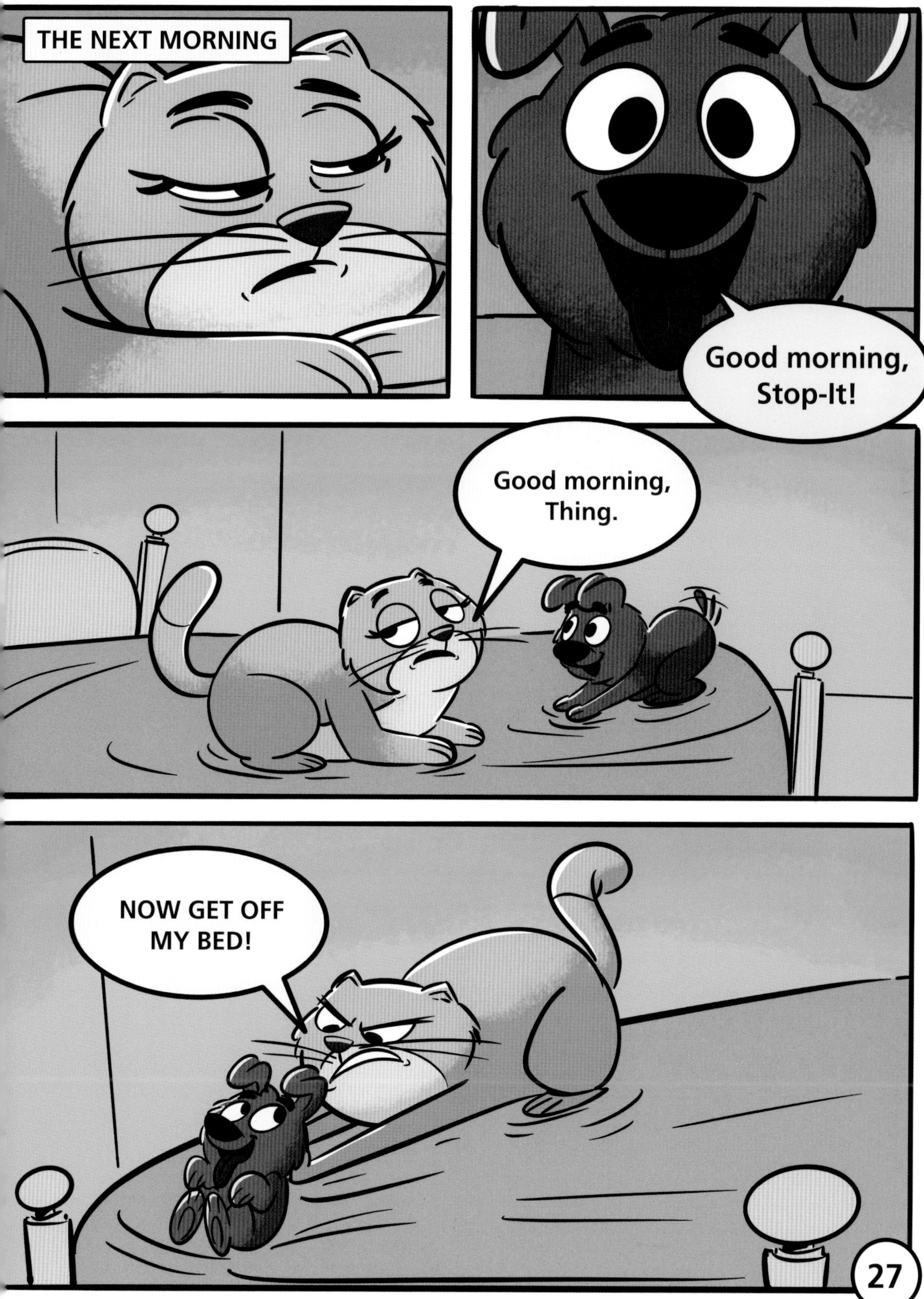
THE NEXT MORNING
Good morning, Stop-It!
Good morning, Thing.
NOW GET OFF MY BED!

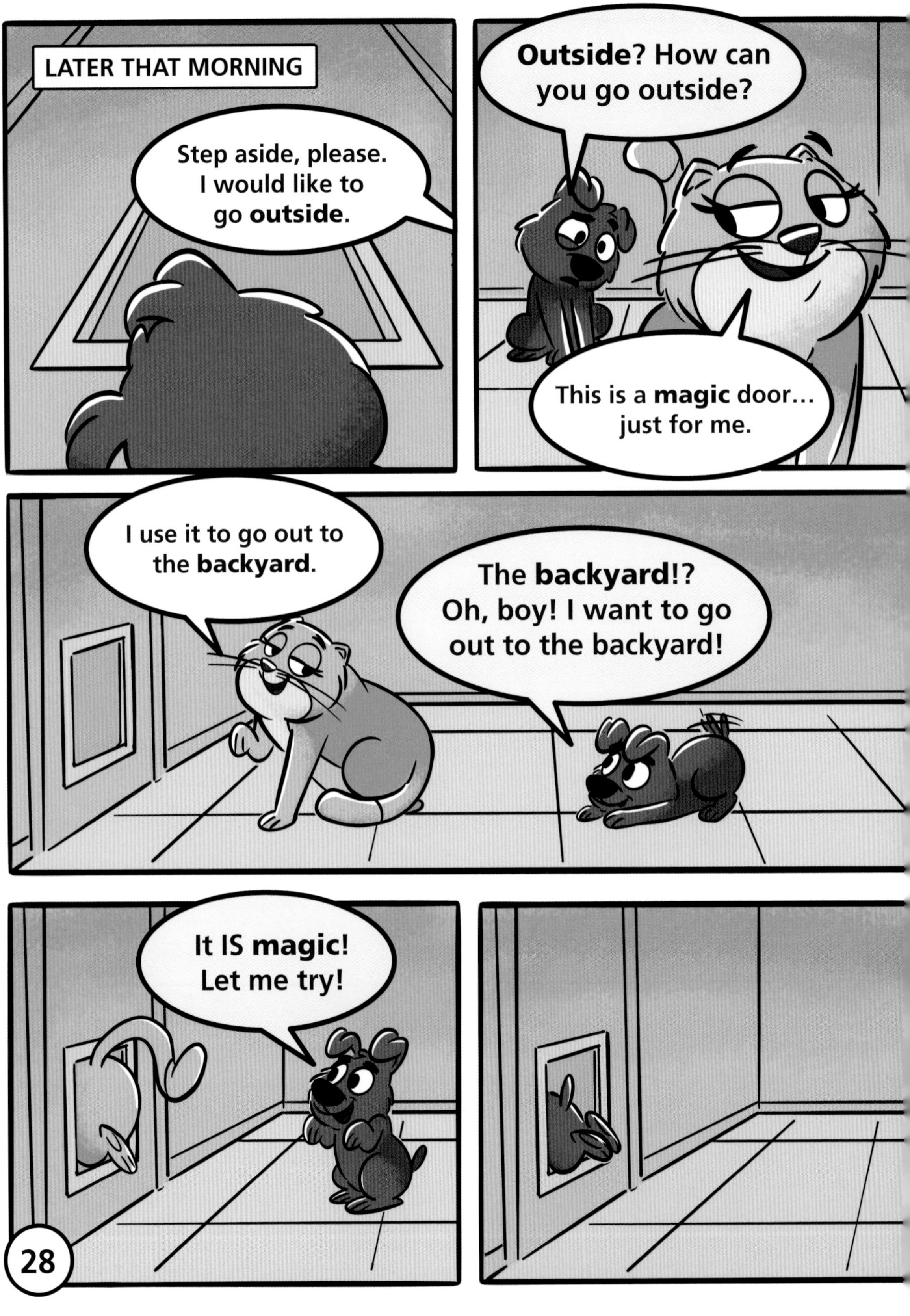
LATER THAT MORNING
Step aside, please. I would like to go **outside**.
Outside? How can you go outside?
This is a **magic** door... just for me.
I use it to go out to the **backyard**.
The **backyard**!? Oh, boy! I want to go out to the backyard!
It IS **magic**! Let me try!

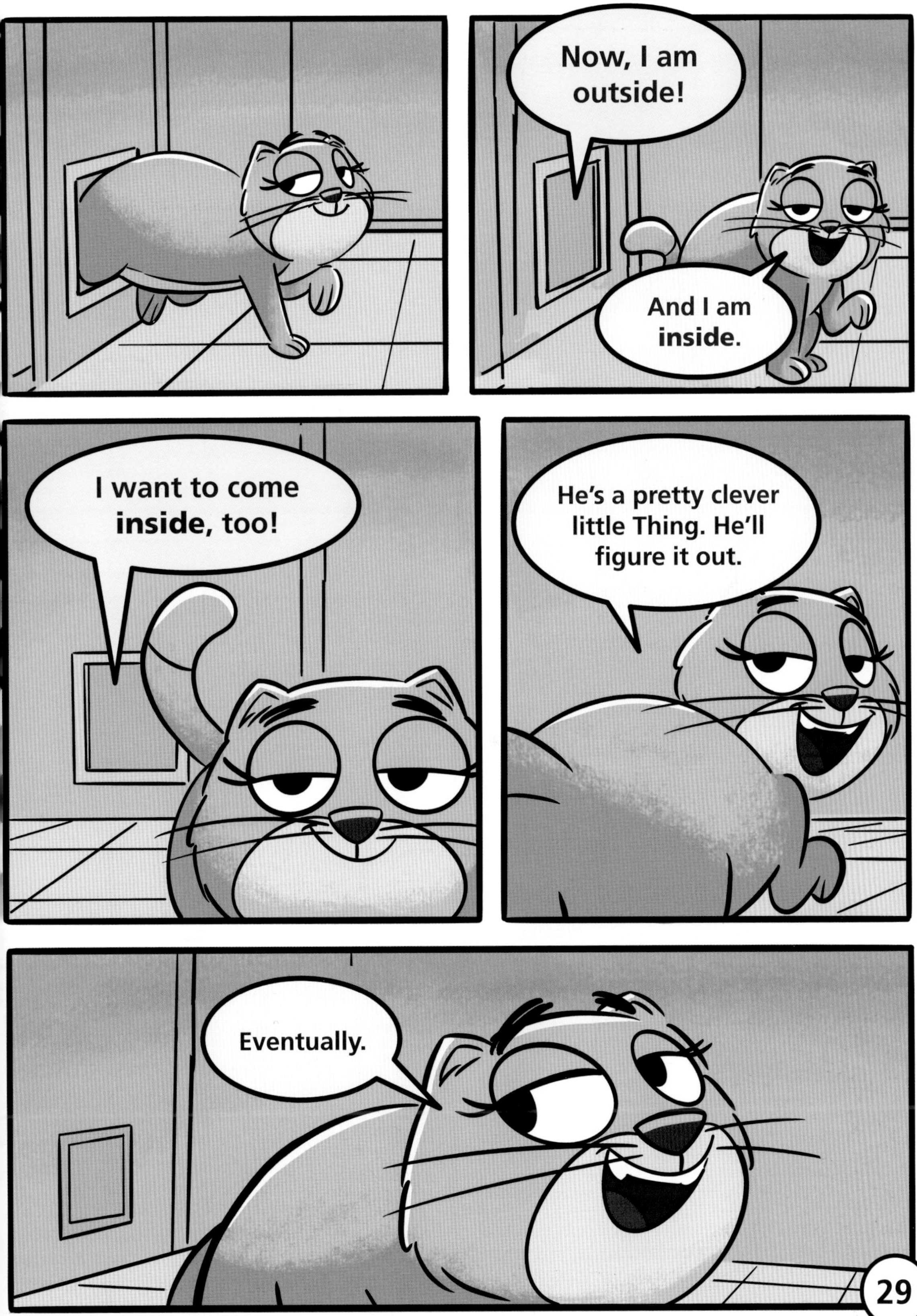
Now, I am outside!
And I am **inside**.
I want to come **inside**, too!
He's a pretty clever little Thing. He'll figure it out.
Eventually.

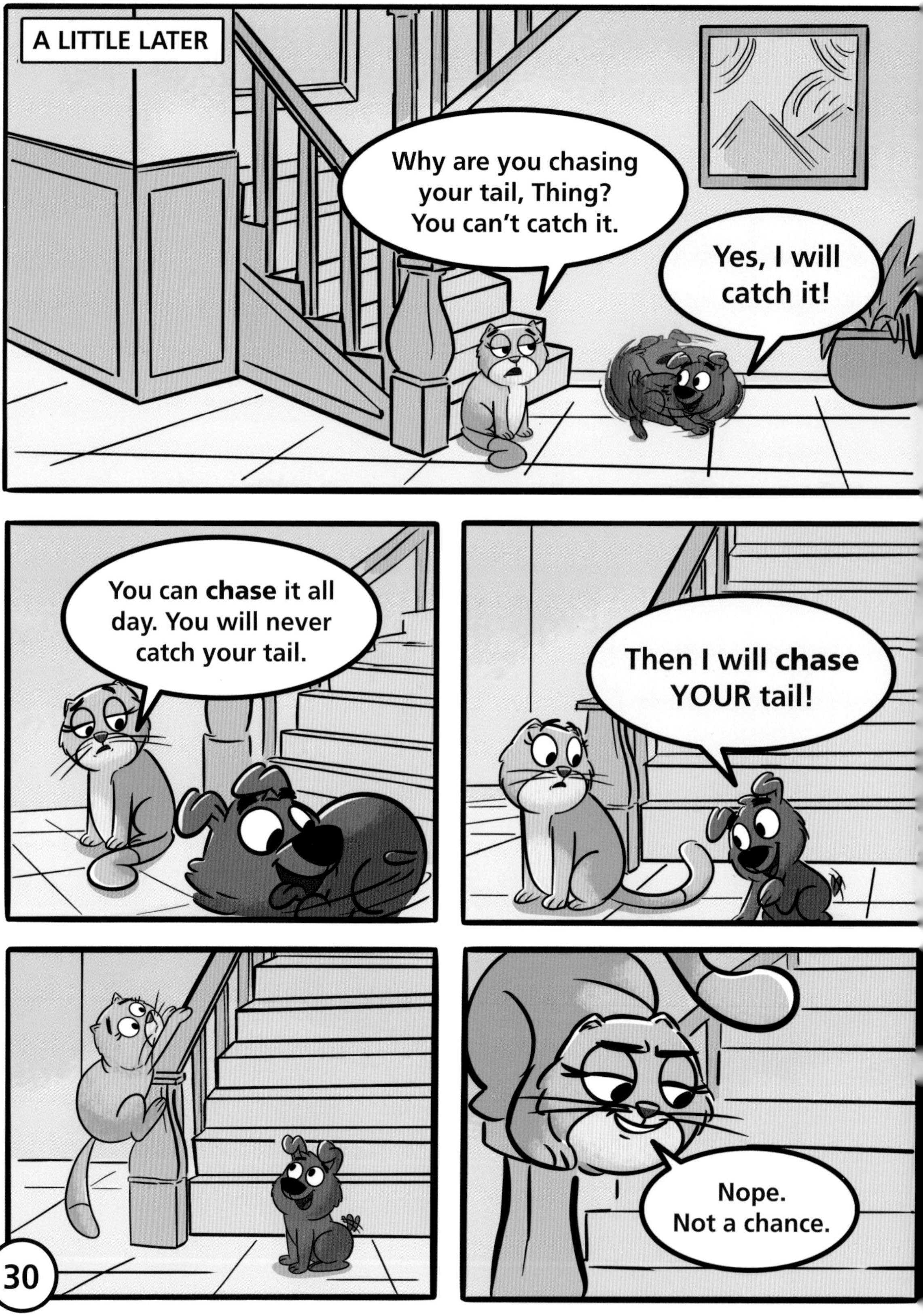
A LITTLE LATER
Why are you chasing your tail, Thing? You can't catch it.
Yes, I will catch it!
You can **chase** it all day. You will never catch your tail.
Then I will **chase** YOUR tail!
Nope. Not a chance.

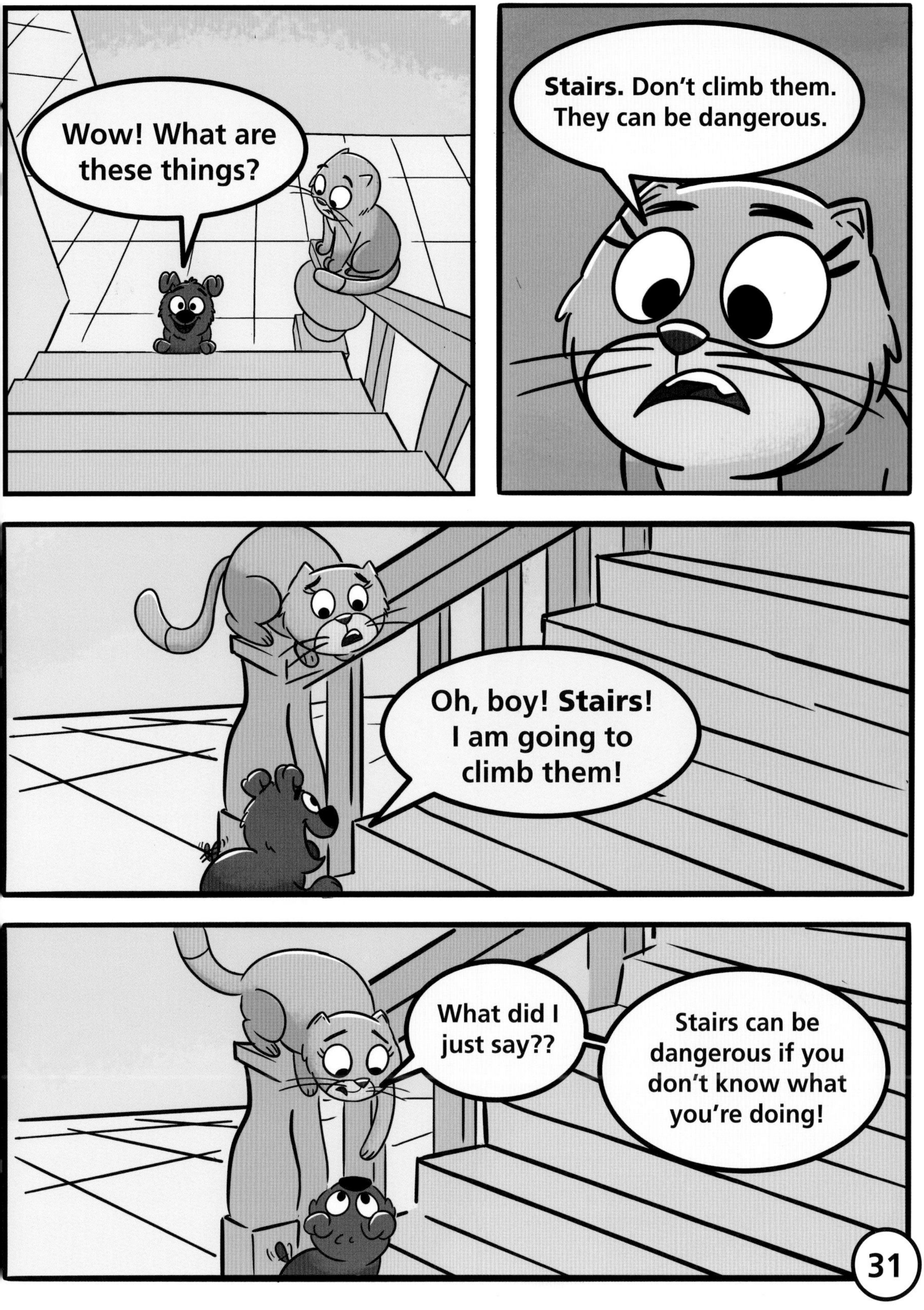
Wow! What are these things?
Stairs. Don't climb them. They can be dangerous.
Oh, boy! **Stairs**! I am going to climb them!
What did I just say??
Stairs can be dangerous if you don't know what you're doing!

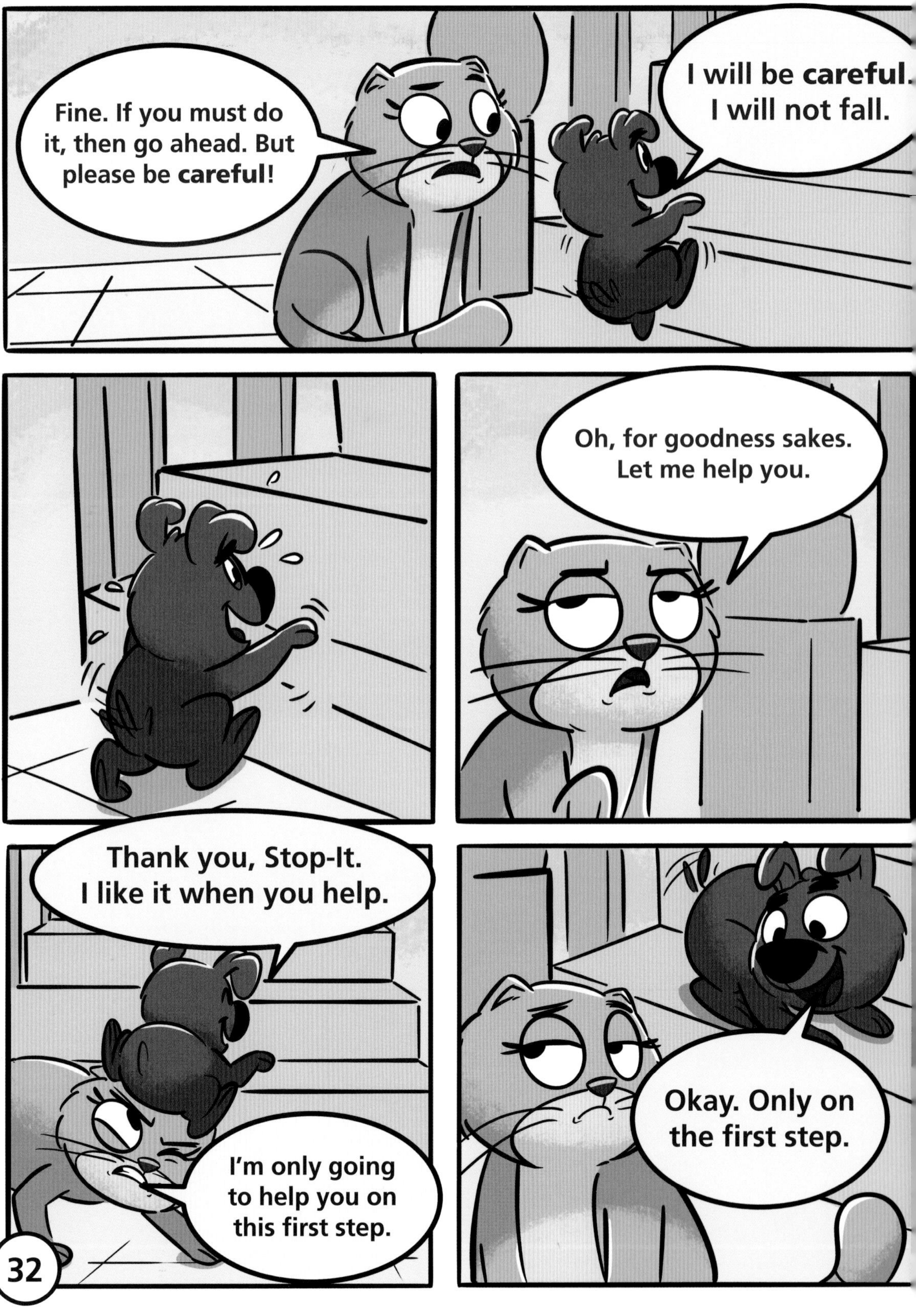
Fine. If you must do it, then go ahead. But please be **careful**!
I will be **careful**. I will not fall.
Oh, for goodness sakes. Let me help you.
Thank you, Stop-It. I like it when you help.
I'm only going to help you on this first step.
Okay. Only on the first step.

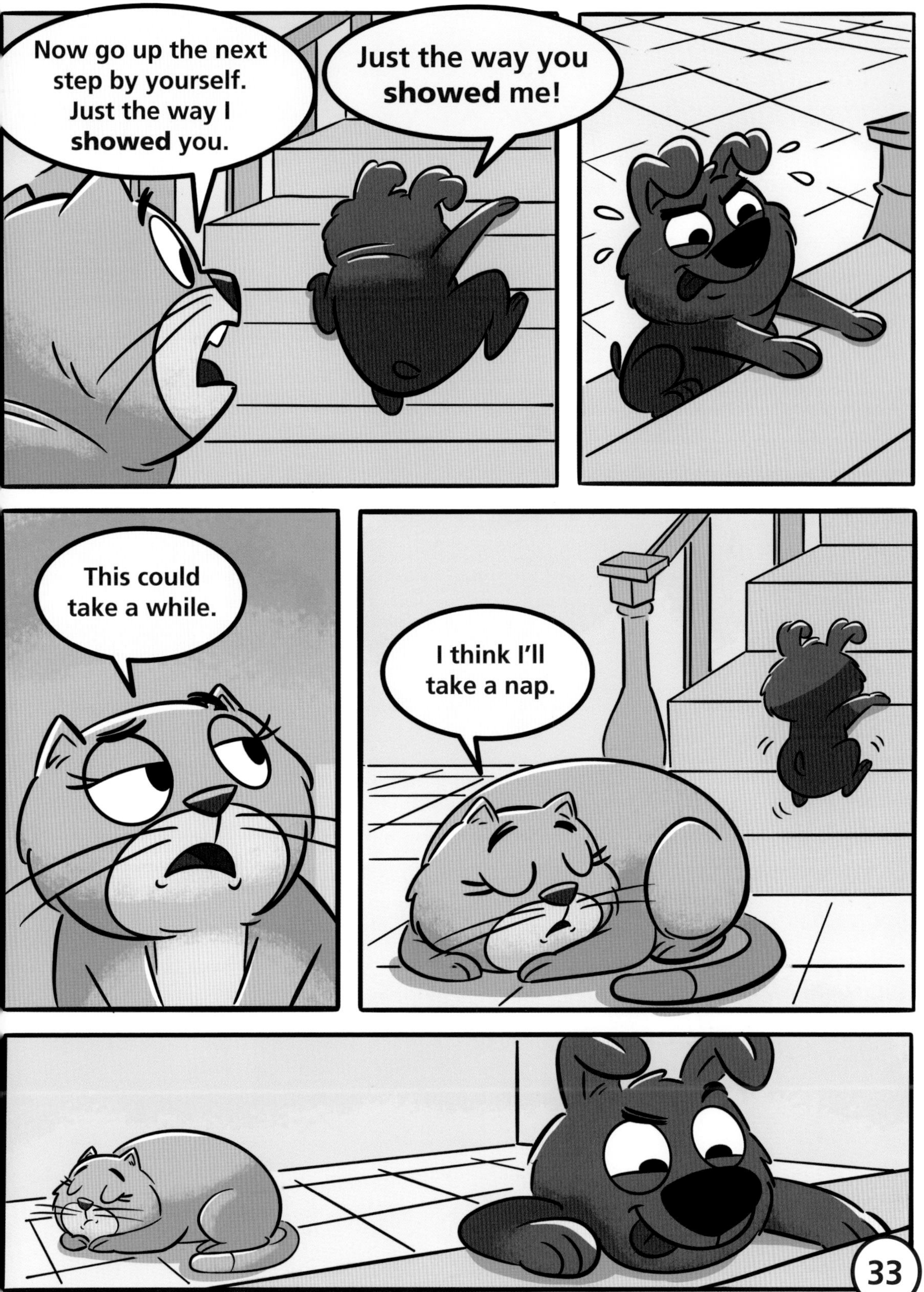
Now go up the next step by yourself. Just the way I **showed** you.
Just the way you **showed** me!
This could take a while.
I think I'll take a nap.

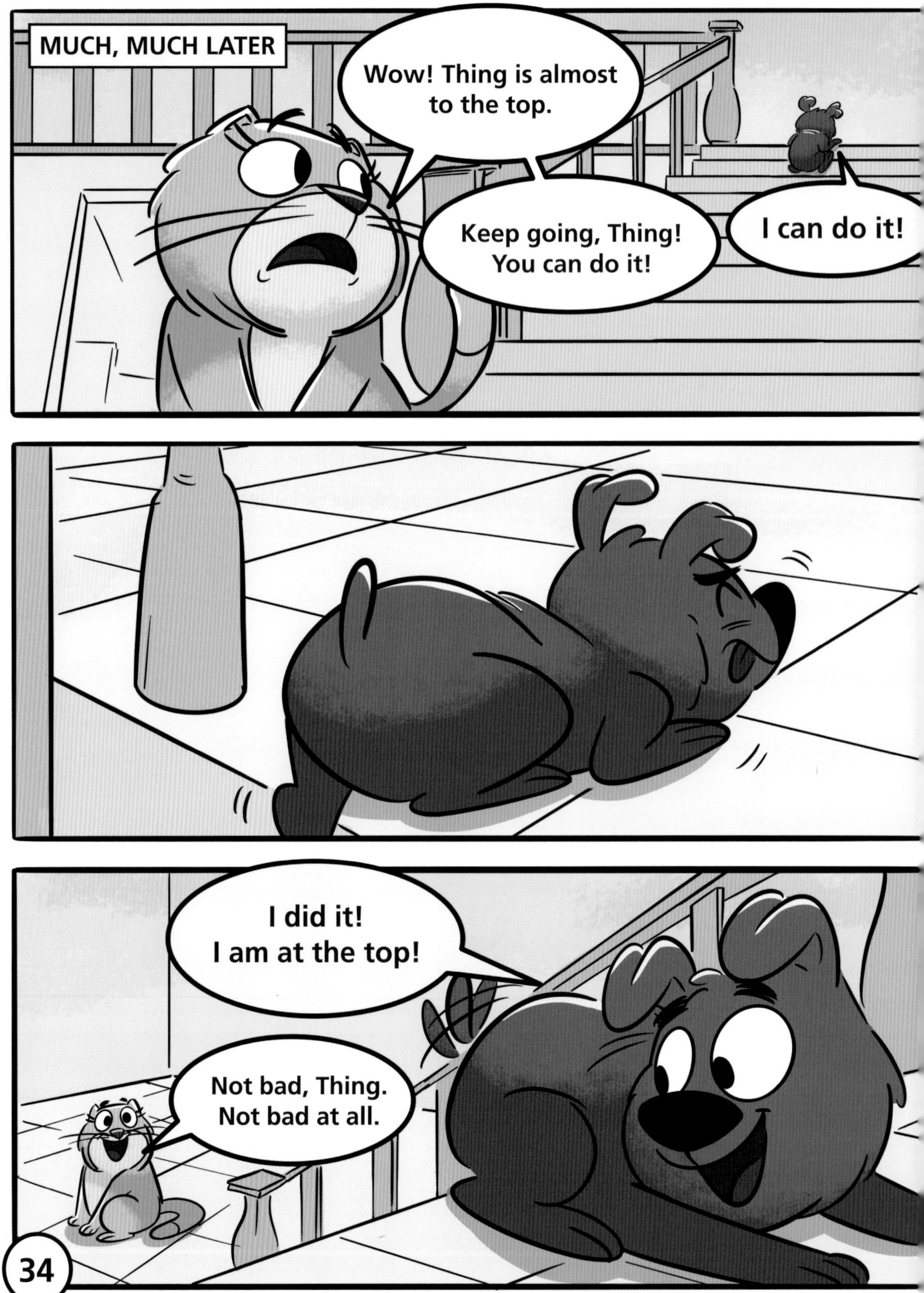
MUCH, MUCH LATER
Wow! Thing is almost to the top.
Keep going, Thing! You can do it!
I can do it!
I did it! I am at the top!
Not bad, Thing. Not bad at all.

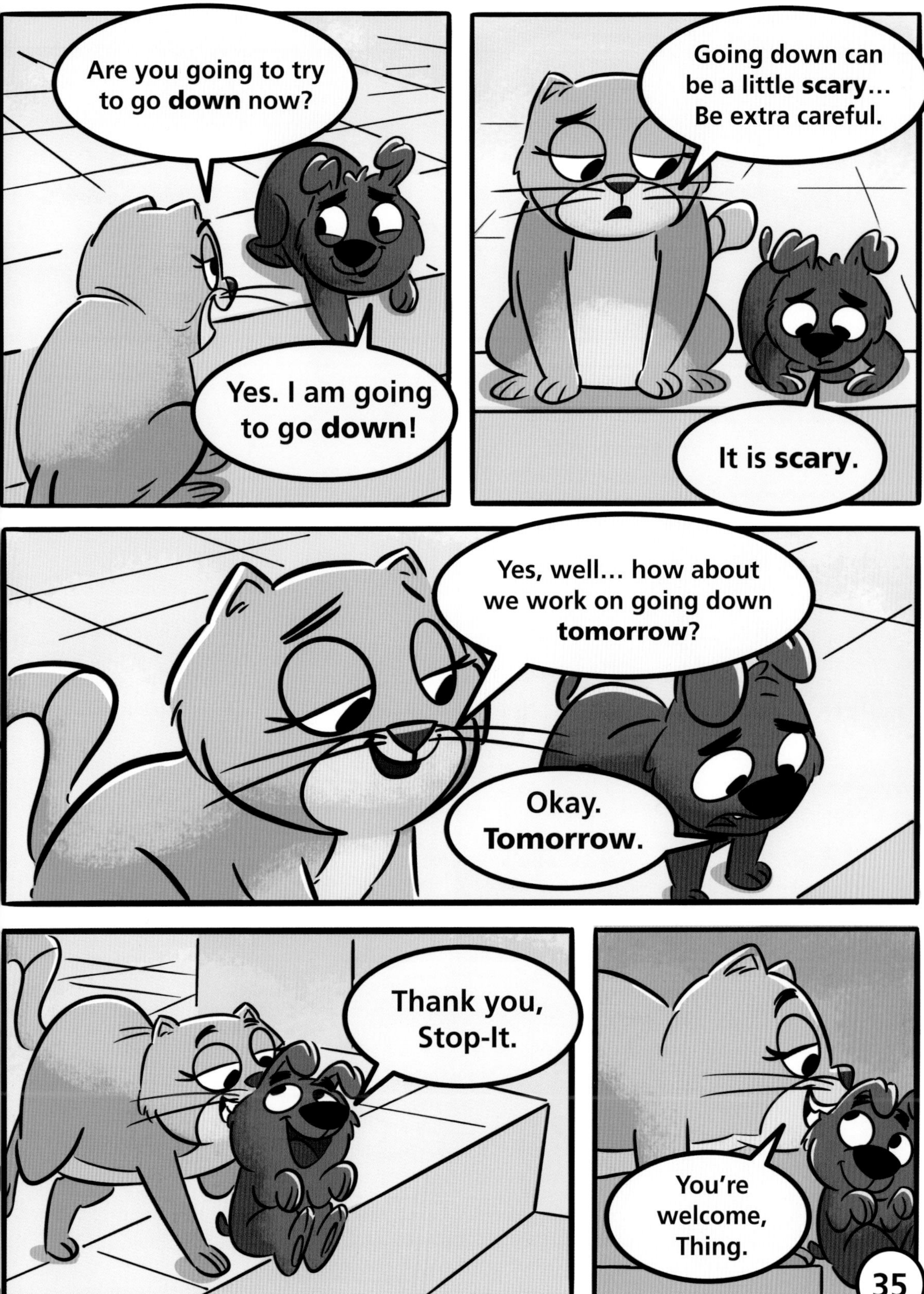
Are you going to try to go **down** now?
Yes. I am going to go **down**!
Going down can be a little **scary**... Be extra careful.
It is **scary**.
Yes, well... how about we work on going down **tomorrow**?
Okay. **Tomorrow**.
Thank you, Stop-It.
You're welcome, Thing.

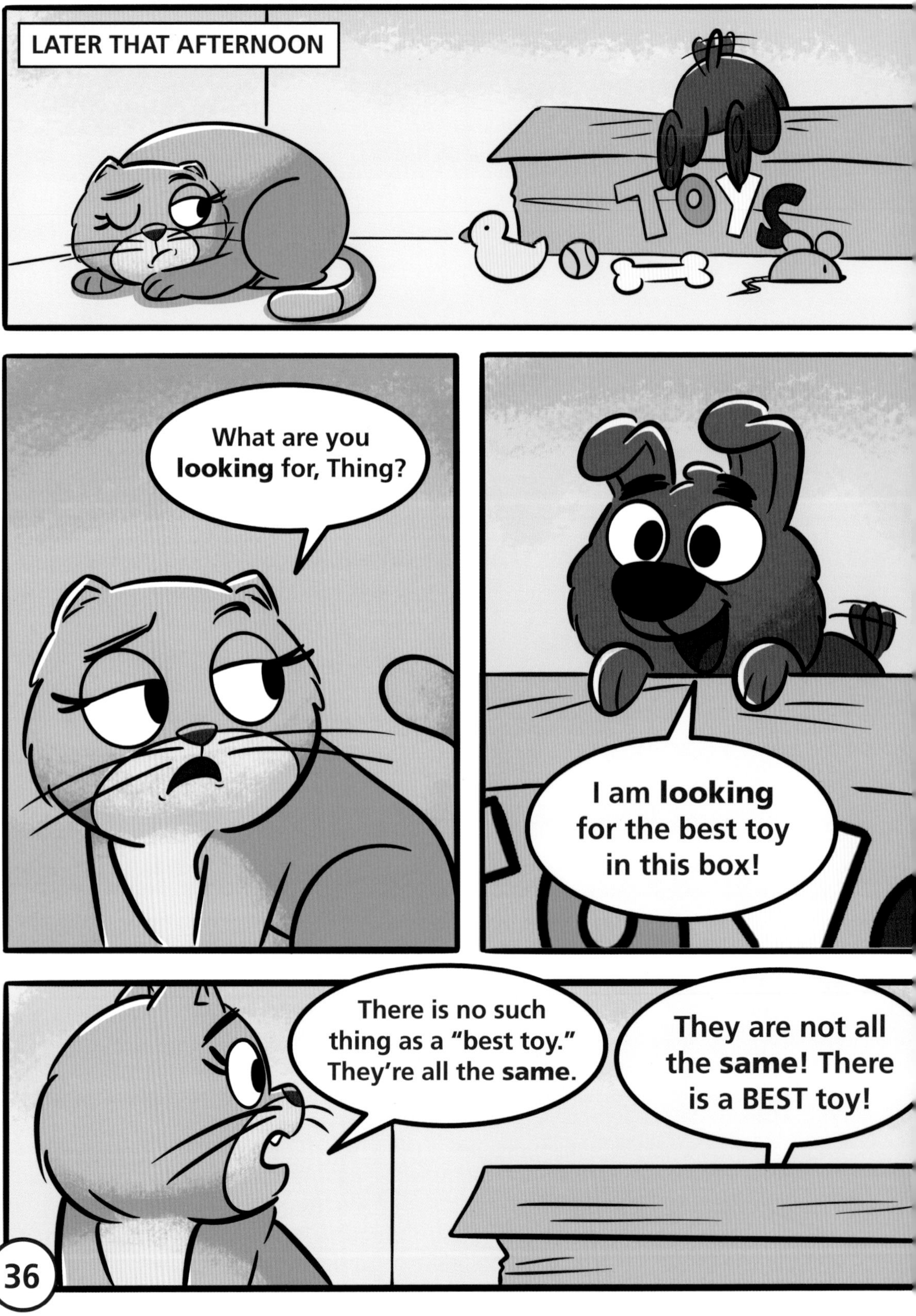
LATER THAT AFTERNOON
TOYS
What are you **looking** for, Thing?
I am **looking** for the best toy in this box!
There is no such thing as a "best toy." They're all the **same**.
They are not all the **same**! There is a BEST toy!

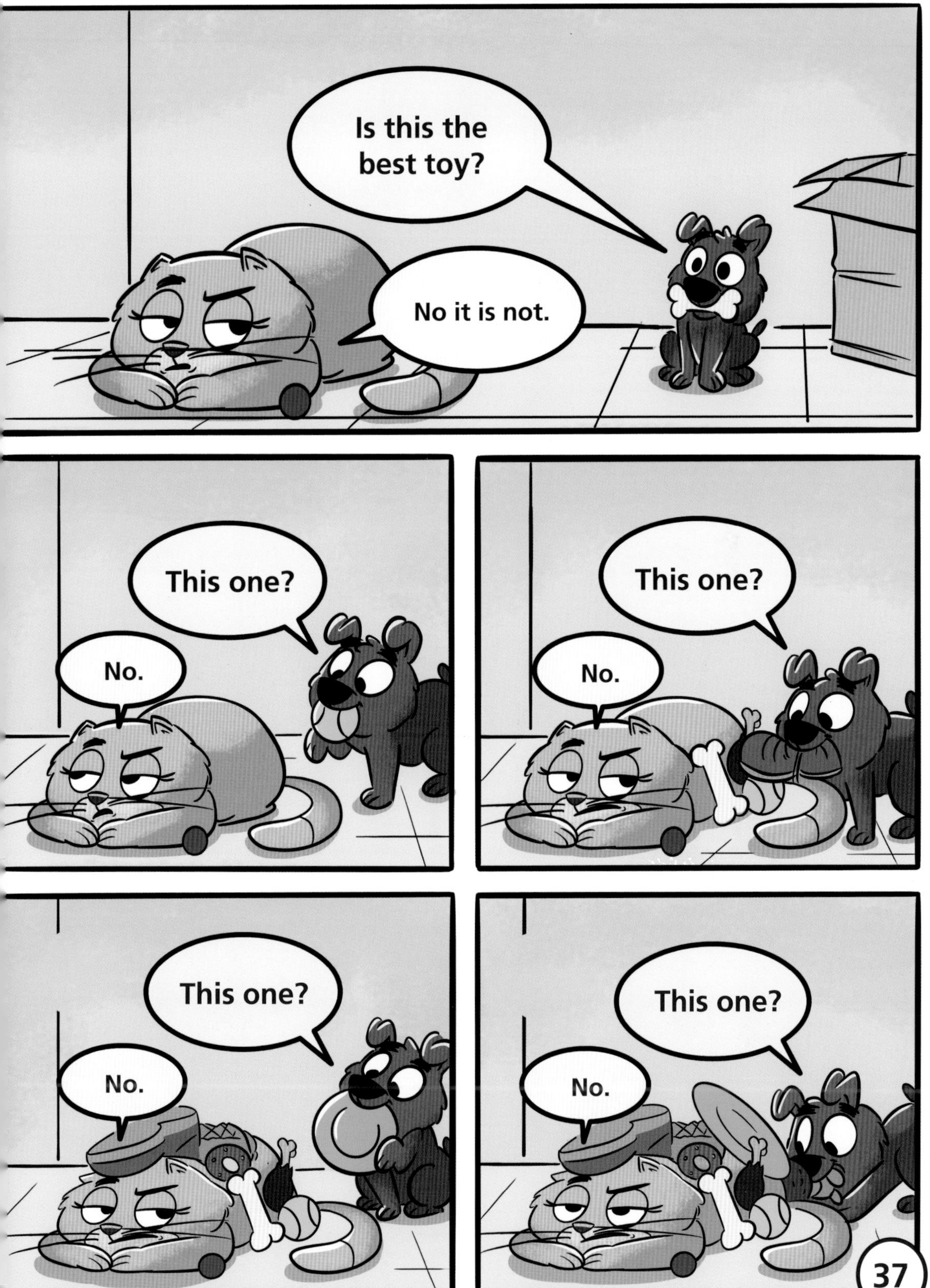

Is this the best toy?
No it is not.
This one?
No.
This one?
No.
This one?
No.
This one?
No.

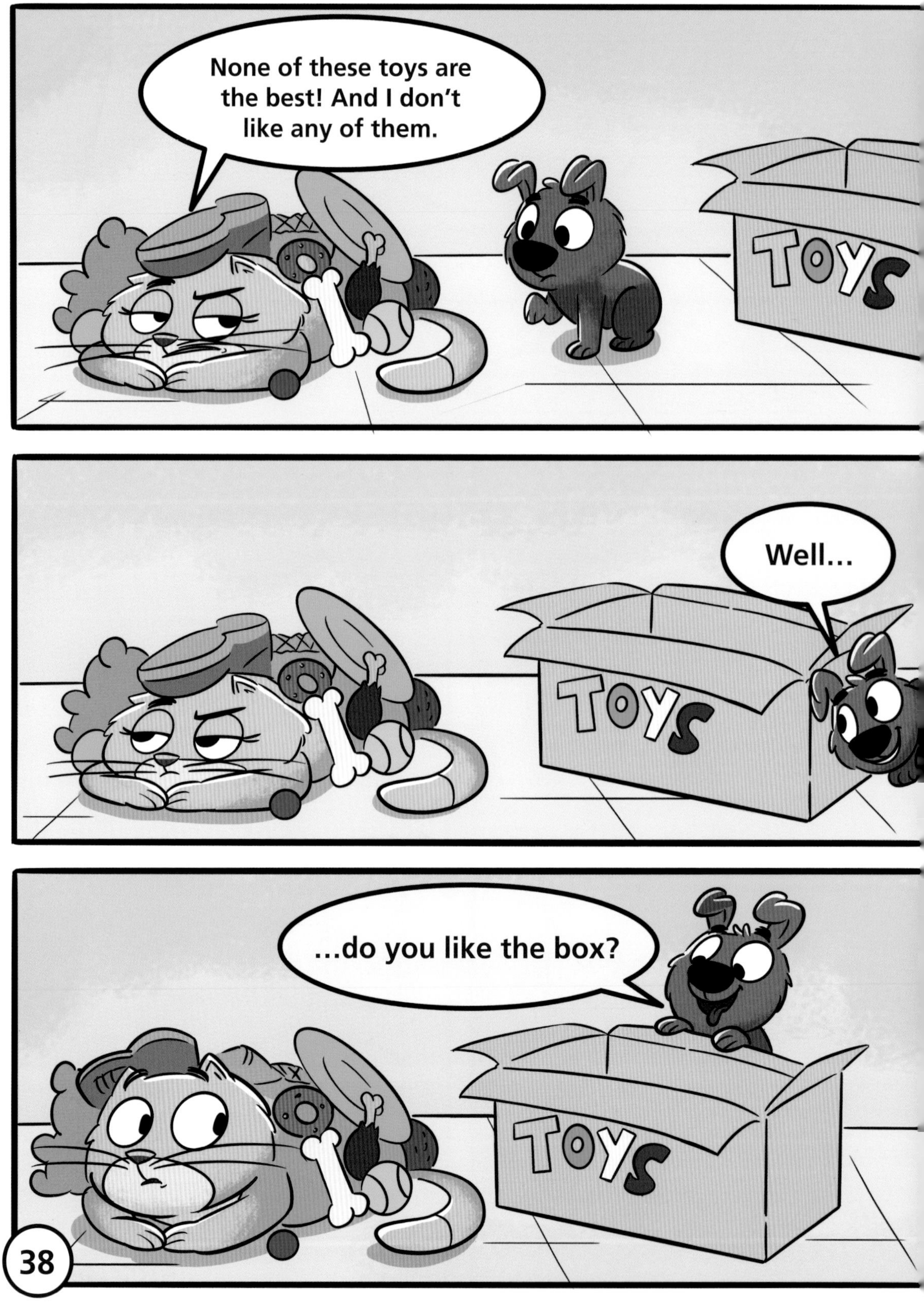
None of these toys are the best! And I don't like any of them.
TOYS
Well...
TOYS
...do you like the box?
TOYS

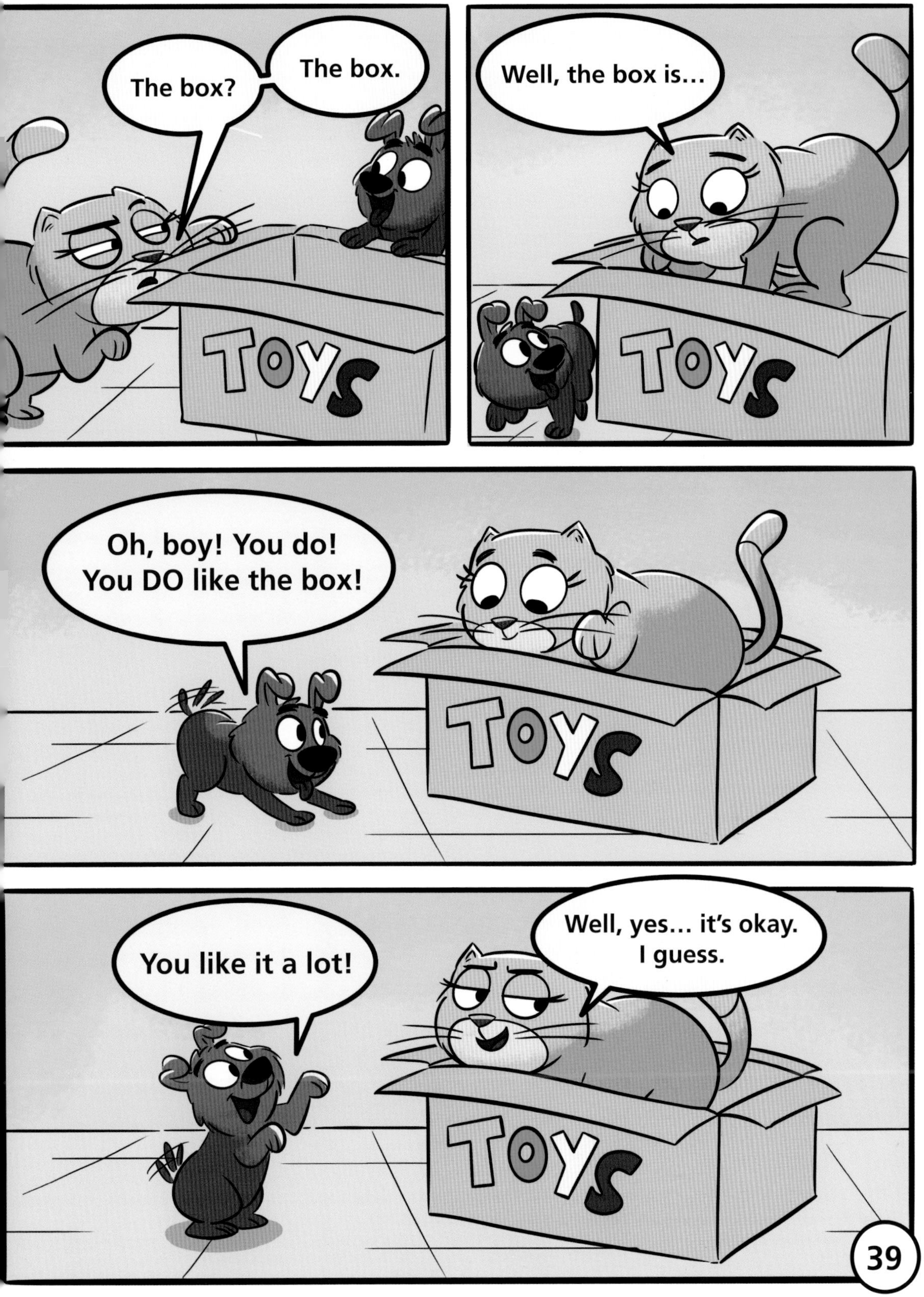
The box?
The box.
Well, the box is…
TOYS
Oh, boy! You do! You DO like the box!
You like it a lot!
Well, yes… it's okay. I guess.

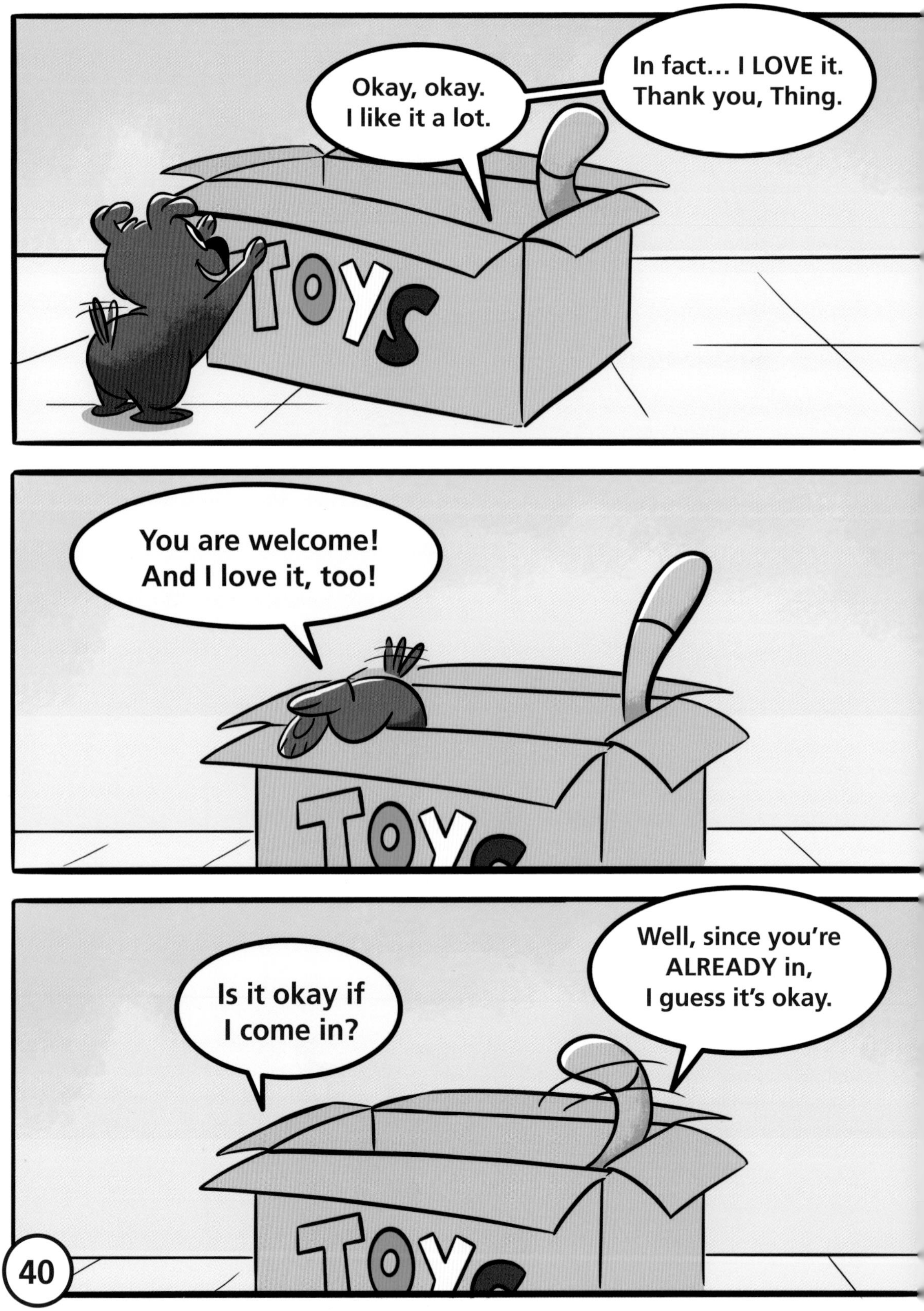
Okay, okay.
I like it a lot.
In fact... I LOVE it.
Thank you, Thing.
TOYS
You are welcome!
And I love it, too!
Is it okay if
I come in?
Well, since you're
ALREADY in,
I guess it's okay.

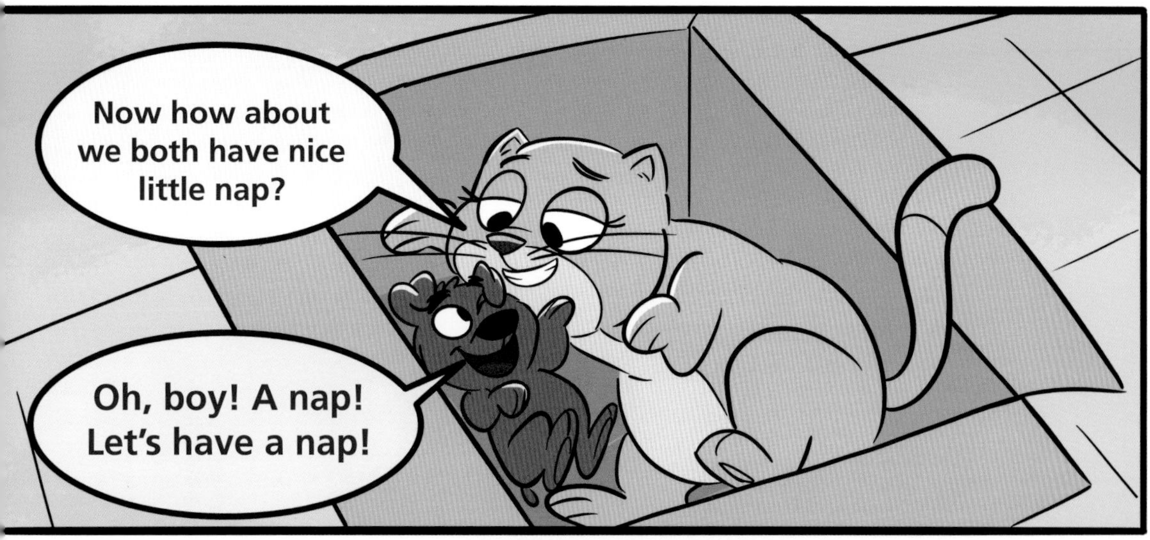
Now how about we both have nice little nap?
Oh, boy! A nap! Let's have a nap!

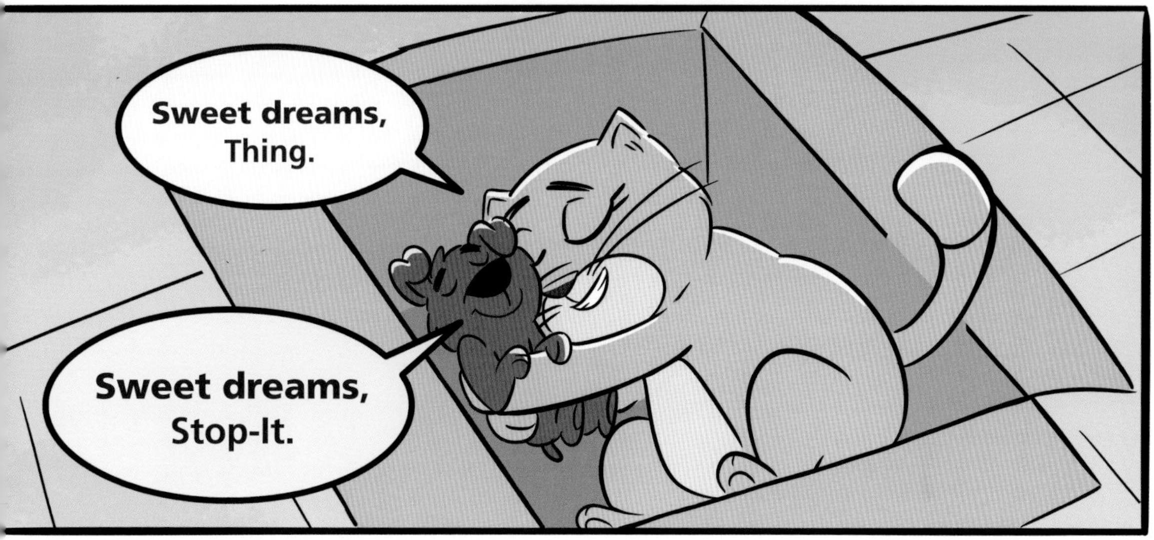
Sweet dreams, Thing.
Sweet dreams, Stop-It.

The End

If you liked ***Thing and Stop-It,*** here are some other We Both Read® books you are sure to enjoy!

WE BOTH READ®
LEVEL 1
The Mouse in My House
By Paul Orshoski
Illustrated by Jeffrey Ebbeler
Take turns reading!
Parent's Page
Child's Page

WE BOTH READ®
LEVEL 1
The Well-Mannered Monster
By Marcy Brown and Dennis Haley
Illustrated by Tim Raglin
Take turns reading with your beginning reader!
Parent's Page
Child's Page

WE BOTH READ®
LEVEL 1
The Emperor's New Clothes
Adapted by Sindy McKay from the story by Hans Christian Andersen
Illustrated by Toni Goffe
Take turns reading!
Parent's Page
Child's Page

WE BOTH READ®
LEVEL 1
About Pets
By Sindy McKay
Take turns reading!
Parent's Page
Child's Page

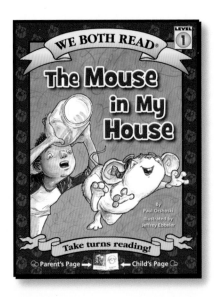

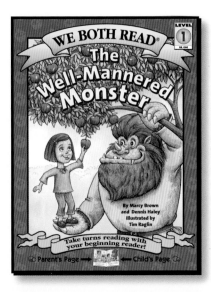

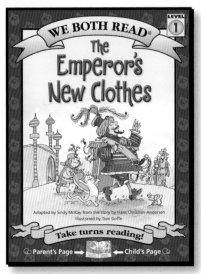

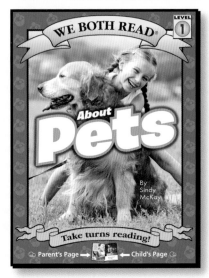